DEPUTY
JOE WHITMORE

A WESTERN ADVENTURE

Russell J. Atwater

Contents

Chapter 1
A Rough Town

Colorado, 1877

The snow-capped summit of Prospect Mountain stood above the alpine forests. Joe Whitmore's horse walked through the forest. The wagon ruts that snaked between the trees provided the closest thing to a trail. The October cold allowed them to see their breath.

Joe continued to follow the trail. He heard the creak of a tree being felled ahead of him. Two lumberjacks chopped at the tree. They paused as they saw Joe ride past.

"Where you headin', mister?" one of them said.

Joe didn't answer.

"That there's the trail to Leadville," the lumberjack continued.

"Mining town?" Joe stared at the lumberjack, who nodded.

"We hoped we'd be sellin' the wood we cut to build the place up," the second lumberjack held his hat to his chest. "Instead, most of what we sell goes into making coffins."

"Right." Joe continued riding along. A gust blew aside his coat, revealing his gun belt. A Colt Army revolver sat in a holster on the left side of his hip, the grip facing outwards for a cross-draw. He noticed the lumberjacks staring at it.

"I hope you're real good with that Hogleg, mister," the first one said. "You're gonna need it."

Joe gave them a curt nod, and they returned to work. He noticed their camp on the edge of the forest, which now gave way to plains. In the distance lay a large tent city, surrounding several clapboard buildings. The Arkansas River skirted the edge of the town.

***

The sun was setting as Joe reached the outskirts of town. A body was hanging from a tree. He heard the rope creak as the body swayed in the wind.

He rode on through the tent city.

A woman in a cheap dress and caked-on makeup stepped out of a tent. She was followed out by a bearded man who was climbing into his overalls. They both watched Joe ride past.

Further down the street, a man in trail clothes sat on a box, spinning the cylinder on a revolver. He spat out a wad of tobacco juice upon seeing Joe's horse walk past. He ignored it.

Joe's horse walked towards Leadville's main street, where the tents gave way to the clapboard buildings. Passersby stepped inside shops and saloons. Some peered out of windows.

A man in a dark suit and top hat nodded to Joe. He nodded back. The man walked over to a yard next to his storefront where two men were building a coffin.

Joe hitched his horse outside a two-story wooden building, signposted as "The Leadville Hotel". He stepped inside, greeted by a smell of rotting wood. An old woman swept the floor, not making any eye contact with him.

An old man sat behind the desk with a hat over his eyes. The movement of the broom across the ground competed with the old man's snoring.

Joe walked over to the man and rapped his knuckles on the desk.

"Who is it?" the old man scrambled out of his chair. He looked Joe over and scowled.

"I'd like a room if you've got one," Joe said.

"Two dollars a night in advance," the hotelkeeper opened a dusty ledger. "Sign here."

Joe took an offered pencil and signed his name. He scattered a handful of coins on top of the ledger. The old man squinted at the name.

"Enjoy your stay, Mr. Whitmore," he said in an insincere tone. "You passing through?"

"Looking for work," Joe said.

"I don't want to know." The old man eyed the Colt Army beneath Joe's coat, along with a holstered Remington on the right side of his hip.

"You got enough for one night. I don't allow any liquor on the premises. Keep this a fine establishment."

As the hotelkeeper handed over a room key, Joe looked around. A layer of dust covered most of the tables and chairs. Flies buzzed around while rats scurried along the floor.

"Right. A fine establishment."

"Martha will show you to the room." The hotel-keeper gestured towards the old lady with the broom. "Any luggage?"

"I travel light," Joe replied.

Martha picked up the key the hotelkeeper had selected. She propped her broom on the desk and walked upstairs.

Joe followed Martha to the second floor. She unlocked a door with a '3' painted on the front. Without saying a word, she opened the door and beckoned for Joe to enter.

He looked inside. A rusty bed occupied the room, along with a dresser, table, and armoire. Martha dropped the key into his hand and walked back downstairs.

Joe stepped inside and sat on the bed, rustling the straw in the mattress. He got up and left, locking the door behind him.

"Where you heading, son?" the hotelkeeper asked as Joe walked downstairs.

"Out for a drink," Joe said. "And some more cigars."

"Keep out of trouble, ya hear?" the old man replied.

Joe stepped outside and looked at the buildings across the street. The signage showed a saloon and a general store. He walked across the street into the general store.

The interior of the general store looked better than the hotel. He noticed a red-headed woman in her early twenties stood at the counter.

Four unkempt-looking men in trail clothes gathered at the counter. One sat on the counter amongst confectionary jars and slugged a bottle of whiskey.

"What's a pretty face doin' in a place like this?" he slurred, amid the laughter of his three friends.

"Please," she stammered, "I have a customer."

"We were here first," another of the men said. "He can wait his turn."

Joe ignored the stares from the other two men as he browsed the shelves. He saw a tin of cigars at the end of the shelf.

"Please stop sitting on the counter," the clerk said.

"Hey," the first man said, "I'm only tryin' to be friendly."

He knocked a jar of jellybeans off the counter, scattering the contents to the floor.

"Oops." The second man chuckled. "Y'know, I hear that Mr. Crawley protects the businesses from this."

"Mr. Crawley has no right to interfere," an older man stepped out of the stockroom. He carried a crutch, which tapped along the ground. "Now leave my daughter alone."

"What are you gonna do about it, old man?" the first man sneered. "Rush to the rescue on that leg?"

The comment prompted an uproar of laughter from his friends. The man kicked the man's crutch from beneath his shoulder. It fell to the floor with a clatter. The junior clerk stooped down to pick it up.

"Get out!" the shopkeeper growled. "All of you!"

"Who's gonna make us?" the second thug spat on the floor. "There ain't no Good Samaritans in this town. You ought to know that by now."

Joe's fist tightened.

"Just go," the clerk said. "If you want money, there's some in the register."

"We ain't here to rob the place," the man on the counter said. "We're just hanging around and having a good time."

The four men laughed as she helped the shopkeeper to his feet and led him towards the door to the back room.

"Aw, don't go," the first thug leapt off the counter. "We only just got here. We were gonna see if your daddy could dance on his good leg."

More laughter followed, silenced by two loud clicks. The shopkeeper re-emerged from the back room with a shotgun. He rested it on his crutch like a stand.

"I said it once and I'll say it again." He said. "Get out before you get hurt. I fought the South, and I can fight a bunch of drunken reprobates without a problem."

The four men paused. They backed away from the counter. The shopkeeper shifted his aim between them.

"Go ahead, gramps," the leader of the thugs said amid a snigger from the second. "There's four of us. You can't shoot us all."

They pulled back their jackets to reveal the six shooters in their holsters.

"You're right," the shopkeeper said. "The first man who so much as touches his gun will get their head blown off. Now, who wants to volunteer for that?"

The four thugs paused and exchanged glances.

"Make your move," the lead man said. "Go on. Give me both barrels. My pals here will shoot you with so many holes you'd be mistaken for a colander. And maybe we can spend some real quality time with Miss Amy there."

His men sneered again. The shopkeeper continued to glance between the four of them as Amy ducked beneath the counter.

Joe stepped forward and cleared his throat. He adopted a combat-ready stance, with his hand resting on his Remington.

The four troublemakers glanced back at him.

"What's it to you, mister?" the lead troublemaker said. "This don't concern you."

"It does when I can't buy cigars," Joe said. "Now, you'd best walk out of here like the man said."

"You got some real gumption," the thug moved his hand towards his own revolver.

"I wouldn't do that if I were you," Joe said.

"You'll regret this!" The leader of the thugs reached for his gun. His three companions reached for theirs.

Joe drew his Remington and fired. The leader of the thugs fell back against the counter. The shopkeeper fired his shotgun and the second thug flew into the shelf, scattering inventory across the floor.

Two criminals reached for their guns. Joe held the trigger on the Remington, slapping down the hammer with his free hand.

Powder smoke filled the room as the sound of gunfire died down. He heard breakage as the two men fell to the ground.

Amy peered out from behind the counter. Joe nodded to her. He looked around. Three of the men lay dead on the floor. The last man crawled away and sat against the wall. He whimpered as he clutched his shoulder.

Joe holstered his Remington and stood over the man, drawing his Colt Army. He cocked the hammer and levelled it at the man's head.

"Please…" the thug raised his hands. Joe's hand trembled.

"Don't do it, son," the shopkeeper said. "There's nothing to gain from an execution."

"I don't want to be looking over my shoulder for the rest of my days," Joe said.

Amy stepped in front of Joe. She grabbed his arm and wrenched it down. The thug scrambled to his feet and left the store.

Joe stared at him through the cloud. He took a deep breath as he holstered his gun. He looked at his shaking hands.

"Thank you for stepping in when you did," Amy said. "I hate to think what would have happened if you hadn't."

Joe said nothing. He forced a smile and gave a curt nod.

"Yes." The shopkeeper limped out from behind the counter. "Those rips have been causing trouble ever since we opened up in this town."

Joe nodded again. He took a deep breath.

"Where are my manners?" The shopkeeper extended his hand. "The name's Silas Coffey. And this is my daughter, Amy."

"Whitmore." Joe shook his hand. "Joseph Whitmore."

"Well," Silas grinned, "you're good in my book, Mr. Whitmore. What can I do to repay you?"

"I just came in to buy some cigars," Joe replied.

"Coming right up," Amy said.

"And I'd be more than happy to buy you a drink," Silas added.

"Yeah…" Joe said, "A drink would sound real good right about now."

"What's going on here?" a commanding voice said.

Joe spun towards the door and reached for his Colt. A stern-looking man with a walrus mustache entered the store, his own revolver drawn.

"I'd stay calm if I was you." He cocked the revolver. "I'm Sheriff Jim McNabb, and I gotta disarm you. Throw up your hands."

Joe raised his hands as he noticed the badge on the man's jacket.

"A couple of fellas had gotten drunk and were harassing my daughter." Silas limped forwards. "When I tried to stop them, Mr. Whitmore here backed me up. Let him be, sheriff. The man's a hero."

"Is that a fact?" The sheriff turned to Joe.

He nodded in response.

"Well, I still gotta take you in," the sheriff said. "I gotta bring it up before the judge in Granite. Your guns, if you please."

"But he didn't start the fight," Amy said. "He did what he had to do."

"I appreciate the sentiment," the sheriff said. "But look at these boys. You recognize them, don't you?"

"I've seen them around," Amy said. "Crawley got mentioned."

"Crawley?" Joe removed his gun belt. "He the big bug in this town?"

"Hudson Crawley," Amy nodded. "He's been demanding a tax from most of the shopkeepers in the town. Those who don't pay get their places smashed up."

"And I'm guessing you ain't paying that tax?" Joe asked.

"Let's go, mister," the sheriff holstered his gun and handcuffed Joe. "Crawley's gonna be giving me trouble if I let you walk."

"Fine," Joe said. "Let's go."

McNabb led Joe out of the store. A crowd had gathered outside. The man in the black suit and top hat approached the store with a measuring tape. The men from the yard followed close behind.

"Step back, folks," the sheriff said. "Go about your business. There was shooting earlier, but it's over now."

"Those are some of Crawley's boys!" someone shouted. "It's about time someone stood up to them blowhards!"

"Don't get any ideas," the sheriff whispered to Joe.

"That fella looks like trouble."

Another man stepped towards Joe and McNabb, flanked by two other men in trail clothes. Joe stared at him. His steely gaze prompted the trio to take a step back.

"Don't get that fella riled," the man with the injured shoulder emerged behind them. "He was real fast."

"We'll be seeing you," he led his companions away.

***

The sheriff's office had a single room with a desk and a stove. A bench with a set of manacles running through an eyebolt sat at the far end of the room.

"Sit down," McNabb ordered.

Joe sat on the bench. The sheriff bent down and secured the manacles to Joe's ankles.

"Okay," McNabb said, "what is your purpose in Leadville, Mr. Whitmore?"

"Looking for work," Joe said.

"What kind of work?" The sheriff's eyes narrowed.

"Anything," Joe said. "Mining or cattle. Something peaceful."

"Something where you don't end up gunning down three men in a store?"

"Something like that," Joe said. "What happens now?"

"We'll be heading to Granite in the morning." McNabb sat down at the desk. "Whether you were a hero or not, you still gotta stand trial."

"Right," Joe rolled his eyes. "Law and order every time?"

"Something like that," the sheriff rested his feet on the desk. "You're lucky I got to you before any of Crawley's boys did. They would have lynched you right then and there."

"Who is this Crawley fella?" Joe asked. "What's his business?"

"He's got a ranch and a few mines," McNabb replied. "Wants to make Leadville his town, and he reckons he's got the pocket full of rocks to do that. He's hiring many unsavory folk to work for him as guards at the mines, but then they get roostered and threaten to shoot up the town.

I'm getting complaints they're demanding protection money from the stores and saloons each month. But I'm just one man and I ain't got a death wish."

"Sheriff McNabb?" Amy Coffey knocked on the door to the sheriff's office. She carried a basket.

"What can I do for you, Miss Coffey?" The sheriff removed his hat.

"I got a couple of things for Mr. Whitmore." She stepped inside and placed the basket on the desk. "I wanted to thank him for stepping in when he did."

"Let's look." McNabb opened the basket. Amy removed the contents: a blanket, a packet of jerky, a small bottle of whiskey, matches, and five cigars.

"That's proper kind of you, Miss Coffey," Joe said as the sheriff moved the items to the bench. "Much obliged."

"You try to keep warm," she replied. "Oh, I brought your horse over from the hotel and gave him a couple of apples."

"Thank you again," Joe gave a warm smile.

She waved as she left the office.

Joe took the blanket and wrapped it around himself.

"Care to join me for a drink, Sheriff?" He uncorked the whiskey.

"Not now," McNabb sat down. "You seem to have made an impression with Miss Amy."

"She seems real nice," Joe shrugged. "Wondering what she's doing in a rough town, but I ain't one to ask."

He took a swig from the whiskey and leaned back against the wall.

Chapter 2
Protection Money

Mal Littler stood behind the counter at Littler's Hardware. He watched his son Pete stack the shelves. He listened to the sound of hooves from outside.

The door to the shop opened. A woman with brown hair entered, accompanied by a younger girl, no older than seventeen years.

"Good morning, Mrs. Hartley," Mal said. "How can I help you and Miss Tina?"

"We have a list." Daisy Hartley produced a piece of paper. "Mostly nails and barbed wire. Our ranch supplies are getting low."

"Of course." Mal studied the list. "Pete, can you help these ladies get what's on the list?"

"Sure thing, Pa," His son replied, taking the list. He exchanged a smile with Tina.

"How are things on the ranch?" Mal asked Daisy.

"As good as can be," Daisy replied. "Ever since Micah's consumption took him last year, we've been trying to keep things going. It's what he would have wanted."

Mal bowed his head.

"Pa!" Pete shouted. His tone carried a sense of urgency.

"Will you excuse me?" Mal said to Daisy. "What is it, boy?"

His son pointed at the open doorway. An enormous figure with mutton chops walked down the street towards the store. Walking beside him was another man, with a neatly trimmed goatee. The second man was in a tailored white suit and tie and carried a walking stick. Two more men, dressed in trail clothes, flanked the pair of them. The rest of the townsfolk fled from the scene.

"Crawley…" Mal's fist tightened. "You ladies had best stay inside and keep your heads down. Pete and I will handle this."

"Pa…" Pete's shoulders tensed.

"It's gonna be fine," Mal walked over to the counter. He bent down beneath the register and produced a shotgun, along with a box of cartridges. "Just stay behind me and let me do the talking."

"Yes sir," Pete nodded.

He loaded the shotgun and snapped it shut before handing it to Pete. He opened another drawer behind the counter and pulled out a gun belt with a holstered Colt Navy.

"Littler!" a booming voice outside said. "Are you in there, Littler?"

Daisy and Tina crouched behind the window and held each other.

Mal stepped outside, followed by Pete. Hudson Crawly and his men stood in front of the store.

"What the hell do you want, Crawley?" Mal's fist tightened.

"Now that ain't very courteous, Mr. Littler," the man in white said with an articulate southern accent. "Mr. Crawley is here to conduct business with you. Something about outstanding tax."

"I know why he's here," Mal said. "He's here because he wants protection money. There's no legitimate tax I owe him."

"Leadville's a rough place," Crawley said. "You winged one of my boys the other day. I can't have that. I need those working for me to be in good shape. Like Mr. Bullock here, my new foreman."

"Lafayette Bullock, at your service," he doffed his hat. "But many around here call me Fate."

"That southern dandy's your new foreman?" Mal smirked. "He doesn't look like he's forked a bale of hay or been down a mine in his whole life."

"That's very presumptuous," Fate replied.

"Enough jawing," Crawley snapped. "This here's my town, and I expect everyone to pay their share. In return, I protect their businesses from the unsavory elements.

But you can't grasp that. You're taking liberties. And I can't have that. So I've come here to prove to the folks of this town that they can't take liberties with me!"

Mal heard Pete cock the shotgun.

"Wait!" he yelled.

Pete levelled the shotgun at Crawley. Fate drew a pair of ivory-gripped Schofield revolvers from his holster and fired two shots. The bullets flew into Pete's shoulder and stomach.

He swung back as the shotgun discharged. One of the Crawley's other men fell to the ground.

"Pete!" Mal drew his Colt and fired at the remaining three men. He ran towards his son, leading him behind a nearby wagon as the men fired at him. Splinters landed beside them as gunfire raked the wagon.

"I got him," the fourth man said. Mal saw the figure approaching the wagon with his gun drawn. Pete breathed rapidly as he handed his father the shotgun.

Mal cocked the second barrel. He fired. The buckshot sent the man flying.

"Mr. Littler?" Fate's voice said through the haze of powder smoke.

Mal peered out from behind the wagon. Fate stood amongst the smoke cloud. He looked around. Crawley had disappeared.

"Mr. Littler?" Fate repeated. "I'm sorry I had to shoot your boy. Is he still breathing?"

"He's hit twice!" Mal called out. "Why do you care, you murderer?"

"I didn't want any trouble," Fate replied. "Mr. Crawley hired me in case there was trouble. Come on out, and we can talk."

Pete looked up at his father and shook his head.

"Where is Crawley?" Mal asked.

"He's out here," Fate replied. "You've shot and killed two of his men already. And you're out of ammunition. Please, I just want to talk. Then we can get help for your son. Are you still watching me?"

"Yes!" Mal called out.

Fate laid his Schofields on the ground by his feet.

Mal gulped. He switched his gaze between Fate and his son.

"Be strong," he whispered, placing a reassuring hand on Pete's shoulder. Pete nodded and closed his eyes.

"What's your decision?" Fate said.

"I'm coming out."

Mal stood up and emerged from behind the wagon.

"It seems you can be a reasonable man," Fate smiled.

Another gunshot echoed through the street. Mal tensed. He looked down. Blood seeped from a wound in his stomach. His legs buckled, and he dropped to his knees.

Crawley emerged from an alleyway, Smoke flowing from the barrel of his revolver. He strode over to Mal, using his boot to push him to the ground.

"You can't get away with this…" Mal said between labored breaths. "I wired a federal marshal some time ago…"

"Shut up." Crawley pulled back the hammer on his revolver.

"If your son survives, I'm gonna give him some time to think about my proposition. But you have cost me, Littler. And I'm collecting what you owe."

He aimed the gun at Mal's head. Mal closed his eyes.

"Goodbye."

Another shot. Silence.

Chapter 3
New Town,
Old Problems

The sun shone through the gaps in the walls of the ramshackle office. Joe groaned as he shuffled on the bench, causing his muscles to ache. He massaged his temples and looked over towards the half-empty bottle of whiskey. The sheriff's footsteps on the floor sounded louder.

"Rise and shine, Mr. Whitmore," McNabb stood over him with a cup of coffee. "It's time to hit the trail."

Joe nodded and moved the blanket aside. He took the cup and clasped it before taking a sip.

"You know," McNabb said, "I always have questions about those who seek comfort in whiskey. If you don't mind me asking."

"I don't mind you asking," Joe said, "if you don't mind me not telling."

"Well, we got a long ride ahead of us," McNabb replied. "We gotta find some way to pass the time."

The sheriff bent down and unlocked Joe's manacles. He stood up and stretched.

The sound of gunfire echoed in the distance. Joe and McNabb both looked in the sound's direction.

"Sheriff!" someone called out. A man charged into the office, panting. "There's trouble over at Littler's Hardware! Come quick!"

"Sounds like I'll be staying put," Joe said. "Unless you need an extra gun hand?"

"No," McNabb pointed at the bench. "I want you to stay put."

He paused for a moment and stroked his chin.

"Fine," he sighed. "You're clearly no friend of Crawley's, since that's who the dirty end of the stick's gonna get pointed at."

He unlocked Joe's handcuffs. Joe rubbed his wrists and nodded to him.

"I'm giving you back your guns," McNabb opened a drawer and the desk and produced Joe's gun belt. "Don't make me regret this."

As Joe fastened the gun belt to his waist, McNabb opened a cabinet behind the desk and produced a Winchester rifle.

***

A crowd had gathered outside Littler's Hardware. Gawkers filled the main street, peering over the heads of those in front of them.

A freighter stood by his wagon with his arms folded.

"Get back!" McNabb gestured at the crowds. They remained standing. He fired his rifle in the air. The nearest onlookers cleared.

The sheriff walked towards the hardware store as the crowd parted. Three dead bodies lay on the street in front of the store. The undertaker Joe had seen the previous day was measuring one body.

"Who are the fellas involved?" McNabb asked.

"This one here is the late Mr. Malcolm Littler," The undertaker gestured to the body he had been measuring. "He's the proprietor of this store. His son Pete is behind the wagon. The other two are strangers whom I haven't seen before."

"Probably hired guns," McNabb said to Joe.

"Any idea what happened?" Joe asked.

"Same thing that happens every day in this town," the undertaker replied. "Mr. Littler and his son had a shootout with these gunmen. Looked like Mal took a bullet to the stomach, then someone shot him point blank through the head."

"Executed," Joe said.

McNabb and Joe stepped towards the wagon near the store. A fourth body, a boy of maybe eighteen years, sat slumped against a wagon, with a gunshot wound in his torso. The sheriff removed his hat and held it to his chest.

"Did anybody see anything?" he asked the onlookers. Nobody answered.

"I didn't come out until the shooting died down," one man stepped forward. "But I reckon it was Hudson Crawley."

"And what makes you reckon that?" McNabb raised his eyebrow. "You see him before the shooting started?"

The man shook his head, not wanting to make eye contact with the sheriff.

"He's shaking you down, isn't he?" Joe said.

The man nodded.

"Who's shaking who down?" A large man in a grey suit approached the sheriff, accompanied by a taller and thinner man in a white suit. The onlooker tipped his hat to them and walked away.

"Mr. Crawley," McNabb rolled his eyes. "What brings you here?"

"I heard there was a shootout in town," Crawley replied. "I wanted to see who was involved and if they were my boys."

"They usually are with you," McNabb glared at him.

"I ain't responsible for what my guards get up to when they're off duty," Crawley turned to Joe. "Now what's this flea-bitten saddle tramp doing here? He killed three of my men yesterday and should wear a hemp necktie."

"Those men were drunk and threatening a shopkeeper and his daughter," McNabb said. "Nobody's lynching nobody until the judge gets told."

"So, he's a gun hand?" the taller man said in an articulate southern accent. "I'm sure we can use a man like him to guard the mine wagons."

"I ain't for hire," Joe spat on the ground. "And I heard plenty of stories about you, Fate Bullock."

"I see that my reputation precedes me," Fate smiled. "As I'm sure it does with you, Mr. Whitmore."

Joe felt his heart beat faster at the mention of his name.

"If you're done here," McNabb raised a hand. "Mr. Whitmore's coming with me to Granite to go before the judge."

"Yet he's still heeled?" Crawley eyed Joe's gun belt. "Your custody seems real lax."

"There was a shootout," McNabb reminded him. "And I figured I'd need a gun hand."

"You seem very trusting for a sheriff," Fate remarked. "But it looks like the shoot out's over. In fact, you could say that Mr. Whitmore was involved. I'm sure Mr. Crawley will offer a generous reward for seeing him brought to justice for the death and destruction he has wrought upon this town since his arrival."

"Keep your money," the sheriff's eyes narrowed. "The judge will decide who's guilty and who ain't. Not you, and not your boss. I'll be looking into this incident deeper when I get back from Granite, you mark my words."

Joe gave the sheriff a curt smile, gaining a newfound respect for the lawman.

"Let's go, Bullock," Crawley cleared his throat. "We got better things to do."

He strode away from the scene.

"Consider your words marked," Fate patted the revolvers on his belt. He doffed his hat to McNabb and Joe before following Crawley.

"You know that tinhorn?" McNabb asked Joe as they watched the two men leave.

"Only by reputation," Joe said.

"Well, who is he?" McNabb gestured for him to continue.

"Colonel Lafayette Bullock," Joe said. "The Gentleman Gunslinger. Cavalry officer or something."

"And how do you know that?" McNabb stared at him. "He seemed to know you. I get the feeling you had a history with him."

"Names like his often get passed around," Joe stared back at McNabb. "It looks like you didn't need my guns for this, sheriff. Shall we make a move to Granite, or am I being released?"

"You're right," the sheriff replied. "We should get moving. Let's hope we don't get dry-gulched on the way back. But since you're under arrest, I'm gonna be asking for those guns again."

"Fine." Joe removed the gun belt and handed it over.

"Sheriff, that you?" another voice said. Joe noticed an older man approach them. He held a stick in front of him, which he felt the ground with. As he drew closer, Joe noticed cataracts in his eyes.

"Is there something I can help you with?" McNabb asked.

"I wanted to come forward," the man replied. "My name's Eddie Ballard. I was going to the hotel for breakfast when I heard the confrontation."

"You witnessed the shootout?" McNabb raised an eyebrow.

"I saw nothing," Eddie pointed to his eyes. "Too much bad liquor. But while I can't see, I heard a lot. Mr. Littler and his son got into a confrontation with Crawley and his men. It was real heated, then I heard shooting."

"I think you need to get your priorities straightened out, sheriff," Eddie said to McNabb, who hushed him.

"Don't worry about the other fella," the sheriff continued. "He's in my custody. But I want to hear more."

"That's about it," A bead of sweat poured down Eddie's face. "I lit out when the shooting started."

He backed away from the sheriff and walked down the street.

"Sheriff..." Joe said.

"I think he knows more than he's letting on," McNabb folded his arms.

"He's afraid," Joe said. "You should make sure he's safe."

"People are gonna be a lot safer when you're out of the way," McNabb said. "Now get moving. We've wasted enough time already."

***

A chilly wind blew as Joe and Sheriff McNabb's horses followed the Arkansas River to the south of Leadville. Through the grey skies, Joe glimpsed the peaks of the Rocky Mountains on both sides of the trail.

"I'm sorry for prying," McNabb said, "but some things you said are gnawing at me."

"Why?" Joe replied, not making eye contact. "Is there another warrant, or do I just match a description?"

"I'm just trying to piece things together," McNabb continued. "You said you're looking for some work that's peaceful. And yet you know a gunfighter like Fate Bullock. I feel like there's a history that I ought to know about. If I don't ask, the judge might."

"The less you know about me, the better." Joe reached into his pocket for a cigar. "Even if I misjudged you."

"How so?" McNabb asked.

"You could have handed me over to Crawley," Joe cupped a match in his hands to shield it from the wind. "But you didn't. Why?"

"I ain't that fella's lackey and I'm not on his payroll," the sheriff looked back at Joe. "I can't have him lynching folk who try to go against him. He ain't the law."

"I always thought it wasn't good to inquire into another man's past," Joe blew a cloud of cigar smoke. "What did you do during the War?"

"I ain't going into that," the sheriff said. "I did things I wasn't proud of."

"Well, I'm gonna say the same thing," Joe replied. "And I'd rather leave it that."

Chapter 4
The Federal Marshal

It was late afternoon when the pair arrived in Granite. Ahead lay a handful of ramshackle buildings, including a post office, a jail, and a hotel. The street was deserted, save for a passing tumbleweed.

"This is Granite?" Joe asked. "Thought it would be bigger."

"Well," McNabb replied, "It's the seat of Lake County, so it's where I keep my office. I got a more secure place to hold scofflaws than I do in Leadville."

Joe dismounted and tethered his horse to the hitching post outside the jail. The sheriff opened the door and motioned him to enter.

The interior of the sheriff's office looked well-presented compared to the one in Leadville. It featured a similar desk and cabinet set-up, along with a stove, but had more chairs. Another door led to the holding cells.

A young deputy sat behind the desk, conversing with a more rugged-looking man. They both fell silent as Joe and McNabb entered. Joe's eyes widened in recognition as he saw the other man.

"Welcome back, sheriff," The deputy stood up. "This here is U.S. Marshal Frank Buchanan."

"Pleasure to make your acquaintance," McNabb offered his hand to the marshal, whose gaze remained affixed to Joe. "I'm Sheriff Jim McNabb, and…"

"And you seem to have brought in Joseph Whitmore," Frank stepped towards Joe and extended his hand. "It's been a long time, Joe. What kind of trouble you been getting into?"

"You know this man?" McNabb's jaw dropped. "He shot three men in Leadville. Killed two of them…"

"We served together in the War Between the States," Frank said as Joe shook his hand. "I always wondered what he got up to afterwards. Perhaps you'd like to explain it? Buy you a drink?"

"Perhaps I will," Joe said, "over that drink you mentioned."

"Marshal," the sheriff scratched his head, "This fella is under arrest for murder. I gotta take it up before the judge, before Hudson Crawley…"

"Hudson Crawley?" The marshal raised an eyebrow. "I'm lookin' for that fella myself. I got a wire from Mal Littler about him. Supposedly he's been demanding protection money from new stores in Leadville, and those who don't pay are getting smashed. Is that a fact?"

"That's the cusp of it," Joe said.

"If you don't mind," McNabb grabbed Joe's shoulder. "I'll handle the talking since it's official business."

Joe glared at the sheriff, who cleared his throat and let go of the shoulder.

"So, what's happening up there?" Frank asked.

"I arrested Mr. Whitmore yesterday in Silas Coffey's general store," McNabb explained. "According to Joe, Mr. Coffey, and his daughter Amy, four men were harassing Amy when her father stepped in with a shotgun. He shot one man, by which point Joe drew on the other three. Killed two of them and winged the third."

"You let him go?" Frank turned to Joe.

"Wasn't planning to," Joe replied. "But Miss Coffey and her old man talked me down."

"What were you doing in the store, anyhow?" Frank added.

"Buying cigars," Joe shrugged. "When do I mention that Mall Littler ain't with us no more?"

"What?" Frank snapped.

"I was heading out this morning to bring Whitmore here when there was a shoot-out at Littler's Hardware," McNabb wrung his hands. "Mal Littler and his son Pete were dead when I arrived. Supposedly, Littler had refused to pay protection money, but only one fella has come forward about the shoot-out and he didn't see it."

"The fella who came forward was blind," Joe added. "Said he'd heard the whole thing."

"Mister," Frank walked up to McNabb and stared at him. "You need to sort your priorities out. Instead of trying to find witnesses to the shootout, you brought in Joe. And it's half a day's ride back to Leadville.

In that time, somebody could have bribed, threatened, or killed anybody who had potentially seen what happened. I'm gonna be heading over to Leadville, and I'll be finishing what you were supposed to. You'd best be ready to head out."

"Told you," Joe smirked.

"Fine," McNabb glowered at Joe. "Just let me get the shootist here into a cell."

"Just make sure your horse is rested," Frank massaged his temples. "I'll deal with Joe myself and sort this mess out with the judge. Trust me, if the situation's as bad as you just said, we're gonna need him."

He walked over to Joe and gestured to the door.

"How about that drink?" he said in a warmer tone. "The hotel here's got some decent whiskey. Pretty reasonable vittles too, and there's a fella you might want to meet."

***

The hotel dining room smelled of sawdust and polish. Two other patrons occupied the tables. A yellow Labrador retriever lay dozing by the entrance. Joe sat at the corner table with his back to the wall. He stared into the glass of beer in front of him. Frank sat opposite him.

"It's good to see you again, Joe," he said. "I've always wondered what you've been up to."

"Nothing good," Joe said. "Surprised to see you on the side of law and order."

"Well, I figured it would let me sleep better at night," Frank took a sip of his own beer. "And it's something where I have to keep my eyes peeled."

"I suppose," Joe said. "Once a fella starts fighting, it's hard to stop."

"So you might as well pick a side you believe in," Frank interrupted. "Maybe you should be a lawman. Taking a fella back to the court can be a good thing."

"Does letting someone else decide if they live or die really help the dreams?" Joe rolled his eyes.

"Joe…" Frank leaned closer. "There's something you ain't telling me. You said something about not planning to let one of those fellas walk out."

"When the lead started flying," Joe took a long gulp of his beer. "I only winged a fella. I was afraid he'd shoot me in the back first chance he got. I didn't want to give him that chance, but I couldn't go through with it."

"It means you're still human," Frank said. "We've all been called upon to kill. But it ain't a thing to dwell on or a thing to relish."

They fell silent as a waitress approached their table with their meals. Joe nodded to her and looked at his plate of steak, potatoes, and corn.

"Much obliged," Frank said to her as she left. "Ain't much variety, but it fills a hole."

"I'm just glad to have a hot meal somewhere that ain't on the trail," Joe cut into his steak and eyed the red interior of the meat.

"Let's talk about the business at hand," Frank said. "What do you know about Hudson Crawley?"

"According to the few townsfolk I spoke with," Joe replied, "He's some kind of big investor in the mines. He's got several gunfighters working for him and probably has the dollars to hire more."

"What kind of gun hands we talking about?" Frank asked.

"Well, the ones I'd confronted weren't much," Joe replied. "Probably some saddle tramps who'd gotten drunk and were looking to shoot something. Dime a dozen. He's got a couple of professionals though. Like Fate Bullock."

"Colonel Bullock?" Frank paused. "He's in Colorado now?"

"From the looks of it," Joe said as he chewed a piece of steak. "You got a warrant on him?"

"I served one," Frank sighed. "But he beat the charges. But he might not beat these. Joe, I got a proposition for you."

Joe stopped chewing the steak.

"It's clear you've seen what Hudson Crawley's capable of," Frank continued. "I know you're looking for honest work and I know you're good with a shooting iron. But you've already tangled with Hudson Crawley, so I got a feeling he ain't gonna let that slide. I was wired by the late Mr. Littler, asking for help with those demanding protection money from him."

Joe swallowed the piece of steak and followed it with a gulp of beer. "I don't like where this is going…"

"You can help yourself by helping me," Frank reached into his vest pocket and produced a star-shaped badge. He pushed it towards Joe's side of the table.

"Deputy U.S. Marshal?" Joe examined the badge and read it aloud.

"I know you too well," Frank said. "You've been running ever since the war ended. You're afraid folks will have less use for your talent as the towns get civilized. But just because you feel they have set you on that path doesn't mean you have to follow it. Crawley needs to be dealt with, but he needs to be dealt with legally. I want to prove to the good folks of Leadville that the law's on their side."

Joe said nothing. His gaze remained affixed to the badge.

"Well…" Frank leaned closer. "What do you say?"

Joe looked at him. "I'll do it."

"I'm glad you will," Frank reached into his coat pocket and produced a small bible.

"You had that ready, didn't you?" Joe smirked.

"I like to be prepared," Frank replied. "You never know when I'm gonna need to deputize folks. Now quit jawing so I can swear you in."

He placed the bible on the table. Joe rested his hand on the book and raised his other hand.

"Repeat after me," Frank said. "I solemnly swear…"

"I solemnly swear…" Joe echoed.

"To uphold the laws of the United States of America. In the face of hardship or temptation, be steadfast and loyal. To protect and serve the people of the United States of America."

Joe repeated the oath.

"Congratulations," Frank shook his hand. "You're now my deputy. It'll be time for you to head upstairs and meet the judge after lunch."

"The judge is based here?" Joe raised an eyebrow.

"Best place for it," Frank replied. "But there's talk of Leadville being the made county seat real soon. Might get an actual courthouse built there. But for now, Judge Panghorn holds his court anywhere that's big enough. And this is the biggest place in Granite."

***

After the meal, Joe followed Frank upstairs but stayed in the hall to give the marshal a few minutes in private with the judge.

Frank stopped outside one door and knocked.

"Who is it?" A voice inside asked.

"U.S. Marshal Frank Buchanan, your honor," Frank replied.

"Come in."

Frank opened the door. Inside was a bedroom with a cluttered desk. A white-haired man in a white shirt and black vest stood by the desk.

A few minutes went by before Frank opened the door to invite Joe inside to join them.

"Joe," Frank indicated towards the occupant, "This is Circuit Judge Clyde Panghorn. He's responsible for Lake County. Your honor, this is Joseph Whitmore who I was just telling you about. We served together in the army, and I've just sworn him in as a deputy."

"Mr. Whitmore," The judge extended his hand. "I heard stories about you. From down in Kansas."

"Dreadful stories, I'm guessing?" Joe felt apprehensive as he accepted the handshake.

"Watch your mouth, Joe," Frank said.

"But I will not worry about that now," Clyde gave a reassuring chuckle. "Good or bad, I know from your reputation and what I heard today that you're handy with a pistol. I could really use a guy like you. As long as you don't get too trigger happy and do what Frank says, we'll get along just fine."

Joe nodded in agreement.

"Now then," Clyde sat down. "You said you were looking for a warrant, Frank?"

"There's some trouble in Leadville," Frank said.

"Of course there is," Clyde leaned back and rested his hands on his torso. "Anything specific?"

"Some fella named Hudson Crawley might be extorting folks in town," Frank explained. "As I mentioned, Joe here dealt with a couple of his alleged flunkies in the general store. I was heading down there myself after getting wired by a fella named Malcolm Littler, who was murdered this morning, along with his son."

"And you believe Crawley was responsible?" Clyde tilted his head.

"So far, no witnesses have come forward about the murders," Frank replied. "But the sheriff informed me that a couple of folks have been paying protection money to Crawley, and that Littler had refused. It's flimsy, but it's the best we've got."

"There was one thing," Joe said. "A blind fella named Eddie Ballard came forward to say that he heard the confrontation between Mal and Crawley."

"He wouldn't have known who killed who," Frank turned to Joe. "But if he recognized Crawley's voice, that would have put him at the scene when the shooting began."

Clyde reached into a leather satchel beneath his desk. He produced a paper and writing equipment.

"Hudson Crawley," he said as he scratched the pen against the paper. "Extortion, and suspicion of the murder of Mal and Pete Littler. You have your warrant, gentlemen.

Now bring him in. I think that Linwood Carrington's staying at the hotel. Perhaps he can serve as the prosecutor."

"With pleasure," Frank took the warrant and folded it in his pocket. "Come on, Joe. Let's get McNabb and ride out."

Joe and Frank walked downstairs. McNabb waited outside with his arms folded. His eyes widened as he noticed Joe's badge.

"I wasn't expecting that," he said. "We riding out?"

"Yup," Frank nodded. "Thanks to Mr. Ballard's statement, we've got a warrant. Joe's been sworn in, so there's less likely to be difficulty when we serve it."

"We?" McNabb scratched his head.

"You know where he'll be staying, right?" Frank asked.

The sheriff nodded.

"Good," Frank continued. "Because you're riding with us."

Chapter 5
The Arrest

"Is Crawley's ranch far?" Frank asked as he rode down the trail with Joe and McNabb the following morning.

"It's about halfway between Leadville and Granite," McNabb replied.

Joe said nothing. He walked his horse after Frank's and watched the overcast skies.

"I still don't get why Joe's with us," McNabb continued. "A gunfighter and lawmen riding together?"

"Same thing," Joe replied. "Only difference is the badge."

"Treat the badge as a reminder of why you carry a gun," Frank replied. "To protect the good folk in these parts."

"Oh yeah," Joe rolled his eyes. "We're cleaning up the West. Just like we cleaned up the South. And look how well that turned out. You know, there are still plenty of folk in Kansas who still want to fight for that Southern Cause."

"The Cause is an excuse," Frank said. "Those fellas are just uniformed bandits."

"They weren't uniformed," Joe said under his breath.

"Sounds like you boys saw the elephant real good back then," McNabb piped up. "Where were you stationed?"

"Kansas," Frank replied. "It was real tough there. Even before the war started."

"What about you, Joe?" McNabb asked. "Were you in Kansas too?"

Joe's grip tightened on the reins. He shut out the chatter, hearing cannons in the distance.

"Joe?" Frank waved at him.

Joe exhaled and looked back at the marshal. The cannons stopped.

"You seemed like something was gnawing at you," Frank said. "You think you can keep your focus when we get there? It's likely to get messy."

"Right behind you, Marshal," Joe said. "Just thought I heard thunder."

"Probably a storm in the distance somewhere," Frank said. "Maybe it'll pass us by."

"Maybe," Joe said. "And sheriff? If we're gonna be working together on this, there's a thing you ought to know. Friends wanting to stay friends never discuss the war."

"We friends?" McNabb asked.

"We ought to be if we're gonna work together," Joe said.

***

The posse followed the trail towards the ranch. Joe heard cattle in the distance. Four men on horseback approached them.

"This here's private property!" one man said. "State your business or ride on."

"I'm a U.S. Marshal," Frank walked his horse forwards. "We're here to see Hudson Crawley."

"Mr. Crawley's busy," the group's spokesman sneered. "Would you like to come back another time or make an appointment?"

"Just take us to the ranch," Frank said. "Or I'll throw you in the hoosegow for obstruction."

Joe rested his hand on his Remington.

"Hey," one of the other riders said, "Ain't that the fella who started that dust-up in Coffey's place?"

"Do you want to obey the badge or the gun?" Joe gave the riders a hard stare.

"He's real fast," the second rider said. "Let's not argue."

"Fine," The lead rider scowled. "Follow us."

Joe followed the group to the main yard, with a barn and a corral, a bunkhouse, and a two-story main house. Four ranch hands stood outside the barn, throwing horseshoes. They cheered as one of them threw a ringer, but went silent as the riders arrived.

Joe exchanged glances at them. One of them ducked into the barn. Another walked over to the bunkhouse. The others continued to watch them.

Another man swept the porch of the main house.

"Hitch your horses by the main house," the lead rider said.

Joe dismounted and tethered his horse's reins to the hitching post outside the main house.

"Let me do the talking," Frank reached into his pocket and produced the warrant.

"Wait here," The spokesman stepped inside the house. The three men flanked the posse as the other men joined them. Joe stared them down. Some men carried guns in hip holsters. The man who went to the bunkhouse emerged, cradling a shotgun. Joe pulled back the lapel of his coat. One man reached for his gun, only for his friend to make a halting gesture.

"Jumpy, ain't we?" Joe pulled a cigar from his shirt pocket. He struck a match against the porch rail and lit his cigar.

"I see the gunfighter is here," Crawley followed the spokesman onto the porch. Fate emerged from the house as well. He leaned against the wall and folded his arms.

"Glad you could join us," Frank said.

"I'm a busy man," Crawley replied. "So speak your piece and get off my land. Have you decided to hand over Mr. Whitmore for killing my employees?"

"You wish," Joe blew out a cloud of cigar smoke.

"I'll handle this," Frank unfolded the warrant. "Hudson Crawley, you're under arrest for extortion, and for the murder of Malcolm and Pete Littler. You gotta ride back with us to Leadville to stand trial."

Crawley chuckled.

"What's so funny?" McNabb asked.

"Just the three of you came all the way out here?" Crawley grinned. "You've got some nerve. Who put you up to this?"

"Circuit Judge Clyde Panghorn of Lake County has signed this warrant," Frank said. "If you've got an issue, take it up with him. But you need to get ready to leave."

"He's not leaving," Fate stepped forwards, resting his hands on his twin Schofields. "You are."

Joe reached for his Remington, when he heard several clicks. The man with the shotgun had pulled back the two hammers and now had it trained on them. The other men had drawn their guns as well.

Joe stared at them.

"I see you have yourself an attack dog, Marshal," Fate nodded towards Joe. "He might have scared the rest of the people there with his fast shooting or his ugly features, but I am unimpressed."

"You're gonna be in a heap of trouble if you kill us," Frank said. "The judge knows we're here and has already wired for more deputy marshals."

"Fate must be eager to duel," Joe rested a hand on his Remington.

"You're proposing a trial by combat?" Fate grinned. "Very well. I accept. Just name a time and a place."

"What are you doing, Joe?" McNabb leaned over to him. "You think they'll let us walk outta here?"

"Enough!" Crawley shouted above everyone. "Lower your guns, men! There ain't gonna be a shout-out today!"

Joe heard more clicks as the men put away their firearms.

"I'll come with you like you asked, Marshal," Crawley said with an arrogant smile. "I got a real good lawyer and I can beat the charges. Nobody saw me commit murder, did they? And extortion? That's just their word against mine."

"Save it for the judge," Frank said.

"Agreed." Crawley snapped a finger and pointed at one of the ranch hands. "Saddle my horse and bring him out here."

"Yes, sir," The ranch hand jogged over to the barn.

Crawley leaned over to Fate. "You know what to do."

"You'd best elaborate on that," Frank said. "It's something that could be considered perverting the course of justice."

"Maybe," Crawley said. "How can I make it worse for myself when you already want to see me in a hemp necktie? But a lot can change before things go to trial. Nobody comes forward in these things. Nobody ever comes forward. This ain't the first time I've had a day in court."

The ranch hand led a horse towards the barn.

"About time," Crawley stepped off the porch and mounted his horse.

"One moment," Frank stepped forwards. He cuffed Crawley's hands behind his back and secured them to the saddle with a length of rope.

Joe stared at the men, who still crowded them. They backed away. As he mounted, he looked over to Fate, who folded his arms.

"Well fellas," Crawley said, "it's time to go to jail. Rest of you, get back to work!"

The ranch hands in the yard dispersed.

"McNabb," Frank said, "You keep an eye on Mr. Crawley there. Joe, you bring up the rear. Make sure his boys ain't following us."

***

Joe said nothing as they rode the Arkansas River trail towards Leadville. Frank rode ahead of the group while McNabb led Crawley's horse along. Joe rode behind, looking over his shoulders as they went down the trail. He trotted up the procession and brought his horse parallel to Frank's.

"Do we really have to take him to that jail?" he asked. "It ain't exactly secure."

"And you'd know," McNabb said.

"Leadville's closer than Granite," Frank replied. "And I don't want to be caught on the trail. Now keep your eyes peeled."

Two riders approached ahead of them. They rode their horses at a trot.

"U.S. Marshals!" Frank called to them. "Keep clear! We're escorting a prisoner."

They moved their horses off the trail. Joe brought his own horse to a halt. He rested his hand on his Remington as the rest of the procession rode on. The two riders kept their distance and rode down the trail. One man tipped his hat as they both left. Joe nodded back at them. He held the reins again and followed the posse along.

"You're Joseph Whitmore, ain't ya?" Crawley asked.

Joe didn't answer.

"I heard about you," Crawley continued. "Even before you killed my people, I heard about you. Stories from the war, and stories from after the war."

Joe tightened his grip on the reins. Crawley looked at his hands and sneered.

"Looks like the dog's getting riled," he said. "What's the world coming to? Giving badges to cold-blooded killers?"

"It takes one to know one," Joe said, not making eye contact with Crawley.

"You're out of line speaking to me like that," Crawley said.

"That's enough out of you," McNabb snapped at him. "I can gag him if you like, Joe?"

"Thanks," Joe gave the sheriff a thankful nod. "But let him let out steam."

"If Mister Crawley feels like talking," Frank said, "Perhaps he'd like to explain what he meant when he spoke to Fate. What is it he knows what to do?"

Crawley chuckled again, prompting McNabb to fidget.

"Anyone who helps me beat the charges gets an extra wage packet," Crawley said. "You'd best think about that."

***

As the party returned to Leadville, miners and shopkeepers flocked outside to watch them ride down the streets. Silas Coffey hobbled out of the general store with Amy. He gave Joe a proud smile and a nod.

Joe tipped his hat to the pair of them and then scanned the crowds for potential troublemakers.

At the sheriff's office, Joe dismounted. He looked around the streets, keeping is coat open so his holsters were visible.

Frank and McNabb helped Crawley out of the saddle and escorted him inside the sheriff's office.

"Is that it?" Crawley grumbled from within. "Just a bench and a bucket?"

"Yup," McNabb replied. "New town, so there ain't a proper jail. And it's more than most people who cross you get."

"This might be a new town," Frank added, "But this state has laws and you ain't above them."

"But I can't live in this pig pen," Crawley said. "What's wrong with a hotel room? My attorney will hear of this."

Joe sat on the decking outside the sheriff's office, smoking a cigar and watching the sunset.

"I'm glad to be out of there," Frank emerged from the office. "Mind if I join you?"

Joe nodded. Frank sat down beside him.

"Cigar?" Joe produced a spare from his pocket.

"Thanks," Frank nodded and took it. "Nice job keeping your head during the ride back. Crawley's lawyer would have a real shindig if he found out we beat him in custody."

"It was just hot air from a buffoon," Joe struck a match against the decking and lit Frank's cigar.

"But he's still raising a few questions," Frank replied. "I ain't gonna ask about it now, but I will ask about it real soon one day."

"When all this blows over," Joe said. "You might have to take me in."

"I'll worry about that later," Frank said. "Right now, Crawley's instructions to Fate have been gnawing at me."

"Agreed," Joe nodded. "What's he planning?"

"I don't know," Frank replied. "Maybe his boys will try to spring him. They've got the numbers, and I don't know when my deputies will arrive. They have the opportunity."

"You think?" Joe said. "He can't deny that, so he'd have to go on the run."

"Maybe," Frank said. "But I know he's going to try something. Until he's sentenced, he's dangerous. We've gotta be ready for anything."

"Yep," Joe said. "Is Carrington due to arrive soon?"

"Hopefully tomorrow," Frank said. "We need people to come forward and testify, though."

"Well, we might have some volunteers," Joe indicated with his cigar.

Silas Coffey and Amy made their way down the street towards them. Silas hobbled on his crutch while Amy provided a guiding arm.

"Keep watch by the jail," Joe stood up. "I'll go talk to them."

He walked towards the pair.

"Good evening, Mr. Whitmore," Amy said with a smile. She noticed the badge on Joe's lapel. "I see you're a lawman now. It's a miracle you took that blowhard in. I hope he rots in jail for all the hardship he's caused."

"Amy!" Silas said. "Let's not air things like that."

"Sorry, daddy," Amy hung her head.

"Don't worry," Joe raised a reassuring hand. "She's right. That fella in there is a blowhard."

"Agreed," Silas said. "And I want to make sure he goes away."

"You're planning to come forward?" Joe asked.

Silas nodded.

"Thank you," Joe smiled. "But be careful. There've been threats."

"Don't worry about us," Silas grinned. "I might have a bad leg, but I still know my way around a gun. Littler was a decent fella, and it wasn't right what happened to him and his boy. I reckon if I speak out, most of the folks around here will. Littler and I were among those who held out when Crawley demanded his so-called tax. I'll ask around."

"Good luck," Joe shook Silas' hand and doffed his hat to Amy. "And you both stay safe."

Joe smiled as he walked back to the office.

"You surprise me, Joe," Frank said. "I ain't seen nobody who could make you smile like that."

"Amy's real sweet," Joe replied. "But I don't know if it would work out. I'm a gambler and a drunk who shoots guns for a living. That ain't exactly husband material."

"What about Anna?" Frank asked. Joe glared at him. "I'm sorry, Joe. I guess it's been too long."

"Forget it," Joe said. "Look, you were talking about the lawyers."

"Yes," Frank said. "You don't want to hear this, but we might have to keep Crawley in the hotel. His lawyer will question the conditions of his cell. Plus, that jail is exposed if his boys do try something."

"I think you're right," Joe said. "Let's get him moved."

Chapter 6
Building a Case

The interior of the Leadville Hotel smelt of sawdust and polish. Joe and Frank sat in the empty dining room the following morning, sipping coffee and listening to the sound of rain outside. Martha placed two bowls of grits on the table. Frank nodded to her.

"Any word on the new deputies?" Joe asked.

"Still nothing," Frank replied. "But I'm hoping Mr. Carrington will arrive today. I gotta admit that the rooms here are probably a slight improvement over the town jail."

"Well, it's nice to sleep in an actual bed for a change," Joe said.

"Excuse me, Marshal," The hotel keeper entered the dining room with a dripping coat and hat in his arms. He was accompanied by a rotund, balding man in a suit and bow tie. "I've got a Mr. Carrington here, said he knew you."

"We've been expecting him," Frank walked over and shook Carrington's hand. "Good to see you again, Linwood. This here's Joseph Whitmore, recently sworn in as my deputy. Joe, this is Mr. Carrington, Attorney at Law. He's prosecuted plenty of folks I brought in."

"Cleaning up the state?" Joe shook the lawyer's hand.

"Something like that," Carrington replied. "Shall we discuss the case?"

"Agreed," Frank offered a vacant chair. "Would you like some coffee?"

"I'm good," Carrington sat down. "They have given me the run-down of the case. Hudson Crawley is facing charges for extortion and possibly murder?"

"That's the cusp of it," Frank swallowed a mouthful of grits. "The murder victims were a hardware store owner called Malcolm Littler, and his son Pete. Crawley had demanded protection money, but Littler refused. Then the shooting started."

"Do you have witnesses to the shooting?" Carrington produced a notebook and pencil, and then scribbled down the marshal's statement.

"We've had someone come forward about the extortion," Frank turned to Joe. "Is that right?"

"Silas Coffey," Joe nodded. "Owns a general store. Also been targeted after refusing to pay protection money. He's gonna get a few other folks to come forward."

"That's good…" Carrington tapped his pencil on the table. "But there's a problem: we're just pitting their word against Crawley's. If you can tie him to the murders, then we have a fighting chance."

"What about Eddie?" Joe asked.

"Eddie Ballard," Frank said to Carrington. "He came forward to say that he heard the confrontation, and would recognize Crawley's voice. But he's blind, and wouldn't have seen the actual murder."

"We can work with that," Carrington scribbled down in his notebook. "But so can Crawley's defense counsel. Him not seeing the gunfight will be a cause for reasonable doubt. We need something concrete. The trial's in a week, and we'll need actual eyewitnesses."

"Mr. Whitmore?" Amy's voice said.

Joe looked up. Amy entered the hotel dining room, accompanied by two other women: A brown-haired woman in her late thirties, accompanied by a teenager of similar features. They both walked with short strides and had dark circles around their eyes. Their dresses were soaked.

"Miss Amy," Joe stood up and walked over to them. "Is there something I can help you with?"

"This is Daisy Hartley," Amy gestured to the older woman. "And her daughter, Tina. They confided in me they had seen Crawley execute Mr. Littler."

Frank and Carrington exchanged a look.

"Why don't you to ladies take a seat?" The marshal stood up and offered the vacant chairs. "Now, perhaps you can tell us what happened. Take as much time as you need."

"We were shopping for supplies in Mr. Littler's store," Daisy said after taking a breath. "His boy Pete was helping us get some things when he noticed Crawley and his men heading up the street. Mr. Littler told us to hide, but we saw the whole thing from the window panel."

Tina burst into tears. Daisy wrapped a reassuring arm around her. Carrington produced a handkerchief from his coat pocket and handed it over.

"I'm sorry…" the teenager wept. "I was just so scared. Ma told me to keep silent in case they heard us inside. And Pete was a real cute boy."

"It's alright," Frank said. "Just try to keep focused. Even the smallest things can be important."

"Okay," Daisy took a breath. "Mr. Littler and Pete stepped outside to confront them. There was a lot of shooting, and a lot of smoke. Pete was hurt pretty bad, but they'd both shot two of Crawley's men. The last fella tried to coax Mr. Littler out. And when he did, Crawley emerged from hiding and shot him. He said he wanted to send a message to the people who tried to defy him. Then he shot Mr. Littler through the head. Tina and I stayed hidden, not wanting to make a sound. We thought they'd come into the shop. When we saw everybody gathering around the bodies, we took our chance to duck out through the back door. Neither of us has been sleeping in case somebody saw us and comes after us."

"Thank you for sharing this, Mrs. Hartley," Frank placed a reassuring hand on hers. "You and your daughter have been real brave coming forward like this. Would you be willing to share this in court in a week's time?"

"I'm willing," Daisy looked at Tina. "But I'm scared. What if Crawley sends men to kill us so we can't testify?"

Joe's eyes widened at her question. He exchanged a glance with Frank, who nodded in understanding.

"We can put you up in the hotel for the week," Frank said. "My office will cover the costs. I deputized Mr. Whitmore there, and I've got more deputies on the way. You'll be safe, and your story could lead to Crawley being hanged if he's found guilty. If you'd like to follow me. I'll arrange for some rooms with the hotelkeeper."

Frank stood up and led the two women out of the dining room. Joe walked them out into the lobby, where Amy was waiting.

"Mister," Frank said to the hotelkeeper, "I'm gonna need another couple of rooms for these two ladies if you can manage that."

"You're pretty much our only guests," the hotel keeper replied. "I'm gonna need more staff."

He led Frank and the Hartley women upstairs.

Joe kept watch at the bottom of the stairs.

"Thanks," he said to Amy.

"Any time," She replied. "I should head back to the store in case daddy needs help."

"Crawley might go after you as well," Joe said. "Ain't you worried?"

"I'll be fine," she replied. "This isn't the first time we've dealt with drunken reprobates causing trouble in our store. Besides, we didn't see the murder, so Crawley wouldn't have any interest in dealing with us."

"Stay safe out there," Joe extended his hand. She shook it and left.

The sound of footsteps prompted Joe to take a position against the wall, giving him a view of the staircase and the front door. The hotelkeeper descended the stairs with Frank.

"All settled in," the marshal said as the hotelkeeper returned to his desk. "I think I know what's gnawing at you right now. Let's talk outside."

The two men stepped onto the hotel's front porch. Rain dripped through the cracks and soaked through the ground. Joe pulled a cigar out of his shirt pocket and offered it to Frank, who declined. The street was deserted, save for the occasional wagon rolling past towards the post office and kicking up the water, which settled in the wheel ruts.

"I get a feeling that I know what Crawley's boasting is gonna be about," Frank said. "You pieced it together from Mrs. Hartley's story, didn't you?"

"Yeah," Joe placed the cigar in his mouth and lit it.

"The Hartley girls and Mr. Ballard are gonna be our key witnesses," Frank said. "If something happened to them, we could lose the case. We need to find Mr. Ballard and make sure we can protect him."

"Is it a good idea to have them under the same roof as Mr. Crawley?" Joe blew out a smoke cloud.

"No," Frank replied. "But we'll take Crawley to the jail in Granite as soon as my other deputies arrive. McNabb and I will keep watch here until then. I'm gonna need you to find Mr. Ballard. Make sure he's safe, then get him to the hotel."

"I'll see where I can find him," Joe looked towards the general store across the street from the hotel. "Reckon Miss Coffey's a good place to start."

"Just don't get distracted from your work," Frank gave him a friendly thump on the back. Joe scowled at him before walking away.

Walking across the street, Joe felt the rainwater soak into his coat and hat. He tossed his soggy cigar into a nearby puddle and stepped into the general store.

Inside, Silas sat behind the counter while Amy swept the floors. The broom strokes provided the only sound beside the click of Joe's spurs.

"Hi Joe," Amy looked up and smiled. "What can I do for you?"

"You have any bottles of liquor?" He asked. "I reckon it's gonna be a chilly night tonight."

"Drinking on duty?" Silas heaved himself upwards. "That ain't the sign of a good lawman."

"It's for later," Joe reached into his pocket for some coins. "But I'm here on business too. I'm looking for Eddie Ballard."

"Mr. Ballard?" Silas raised an eyebrow. "He lives in a shack by the hardware store. Why do you want to see him? Is it about the Littlers?"

"His life might be in danger," Joe said. "I gotta get him someplace safe."

"He's testifying as well?" Amy said.

Joe shrugged.

"To be honest," Silas said, "I don't know if he'd be of interest. He didn't exactly witness the shootout, did he?"

"He still heard it," Joe said. "And he could identify Crawley's voice in court. Plus it was his initial statement that led to the warrant. If Crawley finds that out, he might be looking for some kind of payback on the side."

"That'll be a dollar," Silas placed a small bottle of whiskey on the counter. "Actually, Mr. Ballard might come to you. He often goes to the hotel to take his meals."

"The grub ain't too bad," Joe said. "Does he go often?"

"Every day," Silas said. "He's the habitual kind. Plus, it's the only respectable establishment in this town."

"Well, the owners seemed moralistic," Joe cracked a smile. "Not exactly what I saw as a respectable place."

"Well, there aren't many restaurants around here," Silas lowered his voice and gestured for Joe to lean closer. "Most of those businesses are saloons or whorehouses. I promised Amy's dear departed mother she'd never end up working in a place like that. I want her to make a good wife for someone in the future."

"Can't argue with that," Joe said. "Much obliged for the whiskey and the directions. I'll hopefully see you again soon."

Joe tipped his hat to Amy as he left the store. As he stepped outside, he heard Silas' comments in his head.

"He often goes to the hotel to take his meals. Every day. He's the habitual kind."

The words echoed and repeated. Joe's eyes widened in realization.

"Oh no..."

He ran towards the hardware store.

Chapter 7
Blind Justice

Joe panted as he arrived at Eddie's shack. He looked around. A few passersby wandered the street, finding places to shelter from the weather. He made out a few patrons stood outside the saloon watching him. Joe glared at them. They nodded back or tipped their hats.

Joe looked at the shack. The door was closed. Joe exhaled. He wiped sweat and rainwater from beneath his hat. He took a deep breath and knocked on the door.

"Who is it?" Eddie called from inside.

"It's U.S. Deputy Marshal Whitmore," Joe said. His heart rate slowed as he heard the voice.

He heard the sounds of movement inside. The scrape of a chair. The tap of a cane. Footsteps approaching the door. He heard the key in a lock, along with the sliding of a bolt. The door opened.

"Ain't you the fella the sheriff arrested the other day?" Eddie said. "I thought I recognized your voice."

"They dropped the charges," Joe replied. "They have appointed me a Deputy U.S. Marshal."

"Why don't you come on in?" Eddie stepped back from the doorway. "I'm just brewing some coffee and I'd hate to leave a fella standing out in the rain."

"That'd be much obliged," Joe tipped his hat and stepped inside.

The modest shack contained a kitchen counter, a stove, a bed, and a single chair. There were no lamps or windows, casting shadows everywhere.

"Take a seat," Eddie said.

"I ain't gonna be here long," Joe remained standing. Rain dripped from his coat and hat. He smelled the coffee boiling on the stove.

"So, what's this visit about?" Eddie walked over to a cupboard and produced two cups of coffee.

"Crawley," Joe said. "I need to hear your story."

"There ain't much to say that I already told the sheriff," Eddie picked up the coffee pot as if he could see it. "I heard Crawley shout out Mr. Littler's name. Mal sounded real ornery. He always was a proud fella. There was someone with Crawley. Sounded like a Southern dandy."

"That sounds like Fate," Joe said.

"He introduced himself as such," Eddie poured coffee into the two cups. He handed one over to Joe.

"Much obliged," Joe wrapped his hands around the cup to warm them. "So, they traded words, then started shooting."

"Pretty much," Eddie picked up the second coffee and blew across the top of the cup. "I don't know who shot who, but I heard Fate trying to appeal to Mal to surrender. Then I heard another shot, and Crawley saying 'goodbye' before the last shot. I don't know how long they stuck around for."

"Well," Joe sipped his coffee. "They must have stayed in the area because they were there when I arrived with the sheriff."

"I can't stand Hudson Crawley," Eddie's grip tightened on his cup. "That fella is nothing more than a rich bully. Thinks he can buy the town while it's still being built. Thinks he's above the law."

"You tell a jury what you just told me," Joe said, "and you'll both learn that he ain't above the law."

"I'd love to," Eddie replied. "But I don't think they can consider me an eyewitness when my eyes don't work."

"You still heard what they said," Joe took another sip of coffee. "You could match a name to a person."

"I don't know if I want to get involved," Eddie bowed his head. "What if Crawley beat the charges and found out? He could send his lackeys to kill me. Perhaps even Fate. There was something about that fella that gave me a real bad feeling."

"You let me worry about that," Joe said. "Eventually we're gonna cross a path that one of us won't be walking away from. But if you agree to testify about the incident at the hardware store, I'll make sure you're safe. The trial's next week, and I can put you up in a hotel before then."

"That sounds good," Eddie said. "The hotel in town has a real pleasant restaurant. I head there for my meals most days. Gets me out of the house. But I was scared about venturing out today."

"I'm heading there myself," Joe said. "In fact, that's why I came to find you."

"Well, it'll be nice to have some company while heading over," Eddie smiled. "But do I have to stay in the hotel? That place has stairs. I ain't a fan of stairs."

"I'm sure we can arrange something," Joe said. "The fact is that you shouldn't be walking to the hotel and back."

"Yeah," Eddie downed the last of his coffee. "A fella could get a fever walking in that."

"Or lead poisoning," Joe said. "How often do you go from here to the hotel?"

"Three times a day," Eddie raised an eyebrow. "I know the route like the back of my hand."

"So might one of Crawley's boys," Joe placed a hand on Eddie's shoulder. "A calculating hunter could watch you for a spell and then know your habits. Any place you struggle with on the route?"

"Nothing really comes to mind," Eddie said. "There is one place where my cane gets stuck. Can easily be pulled out, but it's a pain to deal with. Especially when it's raining."

"If they've been watching you," Joe said, "that's a perfect place for an ambush. The sooner I can get you somewhere safe, the better."

"So, you're getting me to move to the hotel?" Eddie asked. "How long am I staying for?"

He reached underneath his bed with his cane, hooking a suitcase handle. Joe finished his coffee and moved the suitcase to the bed.

"A week, at least," The gunfighter opened the suitcase, finding a bundle of clothes. "Until the trial, that is."

***

The rain continued as Joe and Eddie left the shack. Joe watched the street corners as Eddie hauled the briefcase outside, dressed in a rain slicker which smelt stale.

"Can you manage that?" Joe indicated towards the suitcase.

"I'm blind," Eddie locked the door behind him. "I ain't lame and I could still swing a pickaxe. You just keep your eyes open."

Joe nodded. Eddie picked up the suitcase and walked down the street. Joe followed him, checking the street corners. A figure in a wide-brimmed hat and slicker ran past. Joe rested a hand on his Remington. The man stepped into the saloon. Joe relaxed. He walked beside Eddie.

"Yes sir," Eddie said, "I've been prospecting ever since the minerals were first found in Colorado. Made and spent plenty of fortunes until I lost my sight."

Joe gave a verbal nod.

"And things weren't so tense in Colorado like they were in Kansas," Eddie continued. "Few of those border ruffians or jayhawkers."

"Nope," Joe tightened his fist. "I was in Kansas."

"You were?" Eddie piped up. "Then you know what it was like."

"Too well," Joe said.

"Sore subject, huh?" Eddie tapped his cane against a nearby horse trough. "Well, we don't have to talk about that. It ain't right to dig too deep into another man's past."

"Thanks," Joe replied. He glimpsed two men loitering on the street corner, trying to shelter under a shop awning.

"Well, hopefully things will calm down soon," Eddie continued. "And I mean both the weather and the town."

"Yep," Joe maintained his gaze on the two men loitering beneath the shop awning. "Tell me, Eddie, what shops have folks waiting outside?"

"That'll probably be the barber," Eddie replied. "Buford Franklin's the guy. His shop ain't very big, so folks have gotta wait in line on the street."

"Who would go out for a haircut in this rain?" Joe said. He limbered his fingers.

"Franklin ain't just a barber," Eddie said. "He's kind of the town doctor, of sorts. Well, he was an orderly at a field hospital during the war. Got plenty of experience getting bullets out and stitching up wounds. Probably does that more than he cuts hair, if you ask me. This is the town for that."

Joe raised an eyebrow. The two men walked down the street and turned a corner.

Further down the street, Joe continued to keep watch as Eddie continued to ramble. The streets were deserted, save for one or two passersby. Joe glimpsed the two men he'd seen sheltering earlier. They walked down another street corner.

"Darn it!" Eddie shouted. "It's that blasted mud patch again."

Joe turned towards Eddie. His cane had become lodged in soft mud.

"Hold my suitcase, will you?" he said. "I gotta use two hands to get this darn thing freed."

"You'd best make it quick," Joe rolled his eyes as he took the suitcase. "We're sitting ducks out here."

Joe lifted the case, feeling the contents pull his arm down. He saw two men walk out of one building on the corner. He focused through the rain. It was the two men who had loitered outside the barber shop. They looked at him and Eddie and then reached into their coats.

Joe's eyes widened.

"Look out!" Joe dropped the suitcase and shoved Eddie to the ground.

The two men drew revolvers and fired at them. The bullets impacted in the mud. Joe drew his Remington and returned fire. One man fell back. The other man ran towards an alleyway as he continued to shoot.

"Stay down!" Joe yelled. He fired back at the gunman, who fled out of his sight.

"What the hell's going on?" Eddie gibbered. "Is someone shooting at us? I knew it wasn't safe to leave the shack!"

"Keep quiet!" Joe hissed. "There might be more of them out there!"

He snapped a glance back at the first gunman, who lay motionless on the ground.

"Oh great," Eddie said. "I think the mud went up my legs."

Joe exhaled. He walked over to Eddie, keeping his gun trained on the alleyway.

"Some job you're doing!" Eddie grumbled. "You escort me to the hotel and allow me to get shoved?"

"That was me," Joe made quick glances at Eddie and offered his free hand. "You hit?"

"I fell into the muddiest part of that," Eddie said. "I hope you kept my suitcase safe. That thing opens real easy if it's knocked too much."

Joe glanced back at the suitcase. It had opened as it hit the ground. The contents had spilled out and were soaked from the rain.

"We'll get them washed at the hotel," he said as he pulled Eddie to his feet. "Are you shot?"

Eddie patted himself down. "No, I don't think so. I think the mud broke my fall."

"You'd feel it if you were," Joe said.

"My clothes have spilled, haven't they?" Eddie glowered at Joe. "Oh great, now I have nothing dry."

"Well, at least you ain't getting measured for a pine box," Joe said.

Several townsfolk emerged from the houses and shops. Some of them gawked at the dead gunman in the street. Others looked towards Joe and Eddie.

"You okay, mister?" One person approached them.

"Deputy U.S. Marshal!" Joe shouted to them. "Keep clear! There's still a gunman in the area!"

The man raised his hands.

"Easy there," He said. "I just figured you'd need help."

"Run to the hotel and get the sheriff," Joe replied. He continued to scan the crowd for the second gunman.

"Are you going after the other gunman?" Eddie asked.

"I ain't leaving you alone after that," Joe replied. "I gotta get you to the hotel."

"What about my clothes?" Eddie tapped Joe with his cane. "I ain't leaving all my clothes in the mud."

"Mister," Joe said, "You're lucky to be alive right now. I gotta get you to the hotel and then I can get your things together. We're sitting ducks right now."

"What's going on here?" McNabb's commanding voice asked. Joe aimed his revolver in the voice's direction. Sheriff McNabb walked across the decking with the man who had sent for him. He raised a shotgun at Joe as the messenger fled. As they recognized each other, they lowered their weapons.

"Glad you're here, sheriff," Joe holstered his Remington. "Looks like Crawley might be trying to silence Mr. Ballard. Two men tried to bushwhack us. That's one of them over there."

He pointed at the body in the street.

"What about the other one?" McNabb asked.

"Lit out," Joe said. "I had to stay with Eddie."

"We'd best make a move," McNabb said.

"Mr. Ballard's clothes got scattered," Joe said. "Get some of the townsfolk to help you."

McNabb looked at the dropped suitcase, which was slowly filling with rainwater. He swore under his breath.

***

Joe stooped by the hearth in the hotel dining room. He breathed in the smell of wood smoke as he rubbed his hands. He draped his coat and hat on a nearby chair, dripping rainwater onto the floor as he attempted to dry them out by the fire. Eddie sat at one table, tucking into a plate of steak and potatoes.

"Delicious, as always," he said as he cut up the steak. "I'm sorry for getting snippy earlier."

"You were shaken up," Joe replied. "Don't worry about it."

"I gotta say that you handled things real good," Eddie continued.

"You think?" Joe raised an eyebrow. "We ain't outta the woods yet."

"That ain't the point," Eddie said. "Sure, my clothes are gonna need some serious cleaning if they're still wearable, and there's a killer who's still at large. But we're both still breathing. I guess that counts for something."

"Yep," Joe said.

"I see that Eddie's still got his appetite after the earlier incident," Frank entered the dining room and sat in a vacant chair by the hearth. "Ain't you hungry, Joe?"

Joe shook his head.

"What exactly happened out there?" he asked.

"We got bushwhacked," Joe replied. "They were going for Eddie as he got stuck in the mud."

"You think Crawley was behind it?" Frank said.

"That part's obvious," Joe said.

"But you can't prove it, can you?" Frank asked.

Joe shook his head. "One's getting measured. He ain't ever gonna confess."

"You said there was two," Frank folded his arms. "Where was the other one?"

"He got away after his friend expired," Joe said. "I couldn't go after him without leaving Mr. Ballard alone. He can't have gotten far in this weather. I could go after him."

"No," Frank raised his hand. "I need you here. Still have no word on my men from Denver. You and McNabb will have to hang around the hotel and keep a sharp eye out. I reckon this ain't the first shootout you're gonna get into over this."

"Nope," Joe replied.

"Excuse me, fellas," Eddie piped up.

"What is it?" Joe asked.

"I still don't understand how Crawley would have known about my statement," Eddie chewed a mouthful of steak as the lawmen contemplated his words. "I couldn't exactly see him do it, after all."

"You still heard him," Frank said. "And your statement got us the warrant. Best guess is he'll want to make an example of you for going against him."

"That's not what he asked," Joe mumbled to Frank.

"I know," Frank said to Joe. He turned back to Eddie. "There's no way of knowing right away how word got back to him. Maybe they followed us. Or maybe somebody tipped them off. I don't know who'd want to do that though. Most of the shopkeepers came forward about being extorted. You'd think they'd be glad to see their tormentor at the end of a rope?"

"Well, maybe they're afraid he'll beat the charges," Joe stared into the fire. "Or maybe they think they'll be able to buy favors from him."

"Crawley said he'd offer double wages to anybody who helped him beat the charges," Frank said. "He may have started a scramble. I reckon most of Crawley's boys are hired to shoot guns and don't have many other skills."

"If that's the case..." Joe sat back down. "They'd all be tripping over one another trying to get that bonus. Fate's probably gonna try to reel them in. He's the calculating sort."

"You still haven't told me how you know Fate Bullock," Frank said. "I know he has a reputation, but you seem to know a lot more about him than that reputation conveys."

"That ain't important now," Joe looked away from Frank. "Marshal, I gotta clean up and get some rest. You think you can do without me for a while?"

He reached into the pocket of the coat on the chair. Inside was the small bottle of whiskey he'd bought from the general store.

"Sure thing, Joe," Frank nodded. "I'll give you a holler when it's your next watch."

Joe trudged upstairs to his room. He sat on the bed and uncorked the whiskey, sipping straight from the bottle. The liquid burned his throat, but he felt the warmth inside him. He took another swig and corked the bottle, hiding it behind the armoire. He removed his gun belt and hung it on the headframe. Removing his boots, he lay back on the bed and stared at the rotted ceiling.

Chapter 8
The Burning

Joe woke up with a start. He heard a crackling sound in the corridor, accompanied by a piercing smell of smoke. He leapt out of bed and ran to the door.

Smoke filled the hallway. Joe coughed as he breathed it in. A pile of rags had been lit in front of Eddie's bedroom door.

"Sheriff!" Joe yelled between coughs. "Marshal!"

He pounded on the nearby doors. Frank stepped into the hallway.

"That's Eddie's room!" he yelled. "Get him out of there!"

Joe didn't answer. He ran back into his room, grabbing the bedsheet and putting on his boots. He heard Frank knock on another door.

"We need to leave!" Frank yelled. "The hotel's on fire!"

Joe returned to the hallway as Frank escorted Daisy and Tina downstairs.

"Where's the sheriff?" Joe asked.

"Worry about that later!" Frank said. "You need to get Eddie out of there!"

"What in tarnation's going on?" Crawley hammered on his bedroom door. "Get me out of here! The hotel's on fire! You've got the key to my room."

Joe ignored the thumping on the door. He draped the bedsheet over the fire, stamping on it for good measure. The flames died down, but smaller flames emerged from beneath the sheets. Holding his breath, Joe kicked the bedroom door open.

Eddie lay on the floor of the room. He felt around.

"Eddie?" Joe asked.

"Joe, is that you?" Eddie replied. "You gotta help me up. It's hot and I can't breathe."

"Come on," Joe extended a hand. "I'll get you out of here!"

He pulled Eddie to his feet and led him out of the room. Draping the man's arm over his shoulder, he walked him downstairs.

Outside the hotel, Frank sat with Daisy and Tina. They covered their nightclothes with blankets provided by the hotel's owners. The two women held each other in security. McNabb lay motionless on his front on the porch. Several townspeople were running towards the hotel with water buckets.

"He's still breathing," Frank said as Joe looked at the sheriff. "They must have hit him on the head."

"Crawley's still in there," Joe said.

"You're right," Frank replied. "We gotta get him out."

"I'll do it," Joe said. "Stay with the others."

He ran back towards the hotel. Frank whistled. Joe stopped. The marshal threw him a pair of handcuffs. Joe nodded.

Smoke continued to fill the hallway as the fire re-ignited.

"Is someone there?" Crawley continued to shout from within the room. "It's getting hot in here!"

"Get away from the door!" Joe said. "I'm gonna break it down!"

He kicked the door open. Crawley charged out and shoved him to the ground. He ran towards the stairs. Joe grabbed his ankle. The man fell forwards. He kicked at Joe as he scrambled to his feet, and then lumbered down the stairs.

Joe looked towards his bedroom door. He remembered his guns were still there. He tightened his fist and leapt to his feet, running after Crawley.

He ran downstairs. Crawley had reached the bottom of the staircase leading to the lobby. He moved towards a back door. Joe vaulted over the banister, blocking his assailant's path.

"You're still here, killer?" Crawley sneered. "This will be your first taste of hell!"

Joe dodged the hook. He jabbed Crawley in the stomach. Crawley doubled over. Joe followed up with a haymaker.

Crawley fell through a nearby chair. Joe wrenched his arms behind his back and put the handcuffs on his wrists.

"Get up," he growled. "I'm taking you to jail."

Onlookers clapped and cheered as Joe led Crawley outside. Daisy and Tina looked away as Crawley looked in their direction.

"What happened?" Frank asked Joe.

"He tried to make a run for it," Joe replied. "Had to subdue him."

"My attorney will hear of this!" Crawley barked.

"Keep moving," Joe said.

"Where are you taking me?" Crawley said.

"Back to the jail in town," Joe replied.

"Are you serious?" Crawley said. "That's like a dog's kennel. I can't sleep there!"

"Should have thought of that when you offered that bonus," Joe snarled. "Consider yourself lucky. I could have stayed outside and let you burn."

"Why didn't you?" Crawley sneered. "That tacked-on star of yours must have made you soft."

"You might think that," Joe replied. "But that ain't who I am."

"Once a killer, always a killer," Crawley said in a mocking tone. "Try to deny it. I'll pay you fifty dollars to kill whoever started the fire."

"I ain't for hire," Joe said.

After securing Crawley in the prison's shackles, Joe stepped outside the shack. He sat down on the decking and breathed in the chilly night air. The sky was cloudless, giving him a view of the stars.

"Mr. Whitmore?" Amy's voice said. Joe looked up. Amy walked towards him.

"Evening, Miss Coffey," He stood up.

"I saw the fire from my bedroom window," Amy threw her arms around him. Joe recoiled for a moment and then returned the embrace.

"Rough night," he replied. "Looks like everyone got out. Including the guest of honor."

He gestured behind him.

"I heard him shouting," Amy said. "What was he talking about?"

"I reckon one of his men tried to silence our witnesses by starting a fire," Joe said. "It's strange. When I remembered he was still locked in his room, I knew the fire would claim him. I wanted to leave, but I couldn't."

"Your compassion doesn't make you weak," Amy said. "You did what you felt you had to do. It was your duty."

"Yeah," Joe looked at his badge. "My duty. I guess I didn't want to cheat the hangman. Is the barber awake?"

"Most folks would be after what happened," Amy said.

"Good," Joe replied. "Because the sheriff took a nasty blow to the head. I gotta check on the marshal."

"I'll pick up Daddy's shotgun from the general store," Amy replied. "We can keep watch at the jail. Daddy might not be the most mobile fella, but he's still got a soldier's nerves."

"That'd be much obliged," Joe smiled. "Just be careful. This was the second attempt on a witness' life."

Joe walked back to the hotel. Frank walked over and shook his hand.

"Nice work, Joe," he said. "Is Crawley secure?"

"For the moment," Joe said. "But we need to get him someplace more secure. How's the jail in Granite?"

"Better," Frank said. "But we need more men. I don't think Sheriff McNabb will be in a state to help us."

"What happened?" Joe asked.

"Best guess," Frank stroked his chin. "Whoever started the fire must have lured him outside and cracked him on the head. If he survives that, he might not be right afterwards."

Joe scratched his head. "If your other deputies don't arrive soon, we're gonna have our work cut out."

"Tell me something I don't know," Frank said. "And I don't mean about the past."

"We're all clear!" A man stepped out of the hotel with an empty bucket in his hand. "The fire's out."

"That's our cue," Frank said. "Come on, ladies. We can head back inside now."

"You call this safe?" Tina stepped forward. "Someone has just tried to kill us! And don't try to say otherwise!"

"Tina..." Daisy held her daughter. "Please calm down. I'm real sorry about this, Marshal. She's been through a lot. She was very fond of Pete's son."

"I understand," Frank said. "And your apology ain't necessary. We can find safer lodgings for you."

"I appreciate your concern, Marshal," Daisy led her daughter away. "But until you do, I'd sooner take my chances at the ranch."

"Now hold on a moment..." Frank raised his hand.

"I don't want to hear it," Daisy said. "If you find a place, come collect me. But until then, tonight has given me doubts. Besides, I need to tend to the farm."

They walked towards a nearby buckboard.

"You should at least wait until morning," Frank said. "I can't guarantee your safety on the trail and can escort you back in the morning."

"He's right, ma," Tina said.

"Fine," Daisy replied. "We'll stay here tonight. But we'll be leaving after breakfast."

She led her daughter inside.

"What about you, Mr. Ballard?" Frank turned to Eddie.

"I'd sooner stay in the hotel," Eddie replied. "Don't have as far to walk for my meals, and it's a little warmer."

"We'll get you over to another hotel soon enough," Frank replied.

"Do you want me to watch the hotel or the jail?" Joe asked.

"I'll watch the jail," Frank said. "You keep an eye out here. I don't think they'll try anything else tonight. If our firebug was watching, he would have seen that Crawley was in the hotel. They'll most likely be feeling the state if they got any common sense after that."

"Must be one of the desperate ones," Joe said.

"Just be careful," Frank replied. "You never what they're gonna try to pull next."

"Right," Joe offered his arm to Eddie. "Come on, Mr. Ballard. Let's find you another room."

Inside the hotel, Joe led Eddie upstairs, following the hotelkeeper as he opened another room. Once Eddie had settled in, Joe walked downstairs and took a chair from the dining room. He carried it to the hallway and set it down. He returned to his room and put on his gun belt. He extricated the whiskey bottle from behind the armoire and took another swig before returning it. He sat back in the chair in the hallway and folded his arms, maintaining his view on the staircase. His eyes became heavy and his vision was hazy. He leaned back and succumbed to sleep.

A floorboard creaked, prompting Joe to open one eye. Footsteps drew closer. A man stepped into the hallway. He wore a bandana and his hat was pulled low, concealing his face. But Joe felt a cold gaze upon him.

"Mr. Whitmore…" the man said in a gravelly voice.

He levelled his revolver.

Joe leapt out of his chair and drew his Remington.

"Mr. Whitmore?" A softer voice asked behind him.

Joe span round. Eddie peered out of the door. Joe looked back at the hallway. The masked man had disappeared. Joe took several deep breaths.

"You okay there?" Eddie asked.

"It's nothing," Joe rotated the gun's cylinder to the empty chamber. He un-cocked it and placed it back in its holster. "You can go back to sleep. Must have been a rat."

"You must have been having a bad dream," Eddie sighed. "After the events of today, I don't blame you."

"It's…" Joe tightened his fist and then relaxed it. "It's a dream I've been having for a while now. Since the war."

"Some kind of war wound?" Eddie asked. "You take a bullet somewhere?"

"No," Joe replied. "It's one of those scars nobody can see. Go back to sleep, Mr. Ballard. We'll be leaving town in the morning and you'll want to be well-rested for that."

Eddie nodded, closing the door behind him. Joe sat back in his chair and buried his head in his hands.

Chapter 9
A New Safe House

The following morning, Joe's muscles ached as he woke up. He checked the corridor. Empty. He knocked on the door to Eddie's bedroom.

"Who is it?" Eddie called.

"Just checking up," Joe replied. "Let me know when you're ready and I'll get you downstairs."

Daisy emerged from her rooms.

"Sleep well?" Daisy asked Joe, folding her arms.

"It's rare that do," Joe replied. "Did I drop off? Was I snoring? Did I wake you?"

"I wasn't sleeping too well," Daisy replied. "I thought I heard Eddie make you jump. You two were talking outside. So, you were a soldier?"

"I was," Joe said.

"My husband was in the army," Daisy leaned against the wall. Joe offered her the vacant chair. She smiled as she sat down. "He was at Shiloh in '62. There were things he talked about in his letters that he never spoke of after he came home. I can't imagine what he saw there, but perhaps the letter was a mere fraction of what he experienced."

"Where's your husband now?" Joe asked. "If you don't mind me asking."

"Hopefully in heaven," Daisy looked down at the floor. "He died from consumption last year."

"I'm sorry," Joe removed his hat and held it against his chest.

"Don't be," Daisy smiled. "He'd been wrestling with it for a while. Got it from the camp. He decided he wanted to see as much of the world as he could before he left it. When he got older and his consumption got worse, we put down roots around here."

"I guess I'm doing the same," Joe said. "But having a family to do that with must have been difficult."

"It has been," Daisy nodded. "I suppose I liked the sense of adventure. Tina did as well. But it's hard to make friends when you're moving around a lot. What about you? Do you have a family?"

"Not really," Joe said. "They died when I was still between hay and grass."

The door to another room opened. Tina stepped outside.

"Morning, Deputy," She said. "I heard you and ma talking. Are we eating here today? I'm starving."

"Yeah," Joe nodded. "We'll get some breakfast and then the deputy will take you to another safe place."

"I agree," Daisy said. "We should head downstairs. You look like you could use some coffee."

***

The smell of coffee and bacon helped rouse Joe from his stupor. He led Eddie to a vacant table and sat him down. Daisy and Tina sat with them.

"If we stayed with you," Daisy asked, "where would we be taken?"

"Most likely Granite," Joe said. He paused as Martha approached with a pot of coffee. She poured out four cups and distributed them. Joe nodded a thanks to her.

"Is there a hotel in Granite?" Eddie asked. "Do they do good vittles?"

"They ain't too bad," Joe said. "I got taken there the other day. But we've got half a day's ride to get there."

"What did you mean you got taken there?" Tina raised an eyebrow.

"I believe it was relating to that difficulty at Mr. Coffey's the other day," Daisy said. "Amy said you bravely fought off some men harassing her and her father."

"Well, I'm not keen on the idea of a book being written about it," Joe took a sip of coffee. "I've seen too many young men read those and want to be gunfighters. It ain't a thing to choose."

"But you're good at it," Tina said, prompting her mother to hush her.

"This is rough country," Joe said. "Sometimes you gotta be handy with a gun to get far. But it shouldn't be a thing that's celebrated. Taking a life ain't easy. There's a lot of folks who came back from the war with horrible memories. It gnaws at them and often drives them to drink."

He paused. Daisy and Tina gaped at him.

Martha returned to the table with four plates of biscuits and gravy.

"Well," Joe fidgeted, "I don't talk about this much. I hope I haven't spoiled your appetite."

He picked up his cutlery, only to stop when Daisy cleared her throat. He looked up. Daisy and Tina had bowed their heads and clasped their hands.

"What's wrong?" Eddie asked.

"We're just saying grace," Joe replied, copying them.

"Would you like to do the honors, Mr. Whitmore?" Daisy asked. "Or shall I?"

"You go ahead," Joe replied. "I forgot the words a while back."

"Come Lord Jesus," Daisy said, "be our Guest, and let these gifts to us be blessed. Amen."

"Amen," Joe and the others repeated.

***

After breakfast, Joe stepped onto the hotel's porch. He lit a cigar as a group of three riders trotted down the main street, accompanied by two men on a wagon fitted with a cage. Joe watched them make their way down the street. They came to a halt outside the prison. Joe watched them dismount as Frank stepped outside and shook their hands. They carried repeater rifles or shotguns, which they removed from their saddle rings.

Onlookers from the other shops and businesses on the main street stepped outside to observe the newcomers. Two of the riders entered the prison. The third stood by the wagon.

"Mr. Whitmore?" Daisy stepped outside with Tina. They both carried suitcases. "We're heading home."

"You ought to reconsider," Joe turned around and tossed his cigar aside. "Crawley has already tried to kill Mr. Ballard twice, and I reckon his boys would have known about you by now."

"So you've said," Daisy replied. "But if it's just you and the deputy, you'll have a tough time looking after all of us. And I don't like leaving the ranch unattended for too long. Don't worry. We're kind of out of the way and there's only one road leading to the house. We'll spot them if they come."

"It might not just be us," Joe pointed towards the jail. The two new arrivals he saw enter were escorting Crawley to the wagon, accompanied by Frank. They forced him inside the cage and locked the gate behind them.

"You intend to take him to Granite as well?" Daisy leaned over the porch rail for a better view.

"Either that or Denver," Joe shrugged. "I'll ask the marshal when I see him. With any luck, he can have someone watching the house."

"I would appreciate that," Daisy nodded. "I will speak to him about it. Come along, Tina. We must be going."

"Right, ma," Tina said. "Mr. Whitmore, you're gonna make sure Crawley won't get away with this?"

Joe nodded.

"Be careful," Tina said before her mother led her away from the hotel. Joe gave a brief smile.

"What's happening?" Eddie stepped onto the porch, his cane tapping along the wood.

"I think we're getting ready to move out," Joe replied. "You should wait inside until you're called."

"Very well," Eddie shuffled back into the hotel.

Joe watched Daisy and Tina walk over to the marshal. The men removed their hats as they spoke. One man walked away with them. The wagon driver flicked the reins, prompting the horses to trundle forwards. He maneuvered the prison wagon to turn, rolling past the hotel. Joe exchanged a glare with Crawley through the wagon's bars.

"Don't think you've won yet!" Crawley snarled at him. "I'll beat the charges. Then I'll come after you. You'd better leave the county and keep looking back!"

The wagon driver lashed the reins, spurring the horses on.

"Do you hear me, Mr. Whitmore?" Crawly continued to bark, his voice becoming quieter as the wagon moved further away. "I'll make you pay! This is my town, and will keep being my town for as long as I'm breathing."

"Enjoy your new lodgings," Joe said beneath his breath. "You might not be breathing long."

Frank strode down the main street towards the hotel, flanked by the other two men. As they drew closer, Joe noticed the badges on their lapels. One had a bushy moustache and wore a black derby hat. The other had chin-length blonde hair and a wide-brimmed Stetson.

"Morning, Joe," Frank said. "You still awake after last night?"

"Just about," Joe replied. "Crawley was definitely loud enough. These our reinforcements?"

"Yep," Frank gestured to the two men. "Earl Blackburn and Lester Kidd. This here is Joe Whitmore, another duly sworn deputy. The other fella over yonder is Ike Baldwin. I've sent him back to escort the ladies back to their farm."

"Pleasure," Joe extended his hand. "Coffee?"

"That'd be a dandy idea," Earl, the blonde-haired man, grinned as he shook Joe's hand. Lester, the man in the derby, gave a curt nod. "The coffee in this place good?"

"Suits a need," Joe said. "And the owners ain't fond of stronger drinks."

"Then why don't we head inside and we'll fill you in?" Frank said.

Joe followed the posse inside. Eddie loitered in the foyer.

"Okay, this fella here is Eddie Ballard," Frank explained. "He heard the shoot-out at the hardware store and recognized Hudson Crawley's voice. Daisy and Tina witnessed the shooting. They had to return to their ranch."

"I tried to convince them to stay," Joe said.

"Save it," Frank raised a hand. "We can't keep them holed up if they ain't willing. It ain't right."

"It also ain't right to abandon them," Joe clenched his fist. "Crawley's boys have already made two attempts on Eddie's life. They might go after them. It would be better if we could find someplace to keep them together."

"I agree," Frank nodded. "For now, Crawley's gonna be taken to the jail in Granite. We're taking Mr. Ballard to the Granite Hotel, in case Crawley tries something else. He won't have as much clout in that place, so that might take the pressure off us."

"What's the plan?" Joe asked.

"We're taking Crawley to Granite right now," Frank said. "We'll take Eddie tonight. I reckon Crawley drew quite a crowd as we carted him off. I don't want folks seeing us leave. Get some rest, Joe. You could use it. I'll treat the rest of the men to breakfast."

"So, we're not leaving yet?" Eddie asked as Joe led him upstairs.

"Not right now," Joe said.

After taking Eddie back to his room, Joe walked over to the neighboring room and knocked on the door.

"Come in," McNabb said weakly.

Joe stepped inside. McNabb lay in the bed, his head bandaged.

"How you holding up, sheriff?" Joe asked.

"Still seeing double," McNabb replied. "The barber gave me some laudanum for the pain. But I think my days as a lawman are over."

"Do you remember what happened?" Joe asked.

"Not really," McNabb shook his head. "I thought I heard something outside when I came to relieve the marshal. I went to investigate, and someone hit me over the head. When I woke up, the barber was checking me over."

Joe trudged back to his room. Not bothering to take off his boots, he lay down on the bed and stared at the ceiling.

***

A knock on the door roused Joe from his restless sleep. He drew his Remington and heaved himself out of bed.

"Who is it?" He took up a position behind the door.

"It's Frank," The marshal's voice replied.

Joe opened the door.

"Come on," Frank said. "It's time. I've brought your horse over to the hotel, and got a buckboard for Eddie. I want to make good time before sunup."

Joe collected the bottle of whiskey from its hiding place and stepped into the hallway, where Eddie was waiting.

"Still trying to numb the dreams?" Frank gazed at the bottle with a disapproving look. "I'll take that. I need you ready in case anything happens."

He snatched the bottle away. Joe did nothing to stop him. Eddie heard the sloshing and reached for the bottle. Frank glanced back at Joe, who shrugged in response.

"Mr. Ballard," the marshal turned to Joe, "We're moving you to another hotel in case Crawley's men try to start another fire here. But we need to be careful about this. We mustn't make any more noise than we have to. You mustn't say anything for as long as we're out on the trail unless it's real important. Sound carries at night, and you never know who might pick that up. Do you understand?"

Eddie nodded.

"Good," Frank smiled. "And that goes for the rest of you. Now let's get moving."

The group walked downstairs. A full moon was out, with little cloud. Joe followed Frank outside, where Earl and Lester waited with the horses and the buckboard. Joe helped Eddie into the buckboard and mounted his own horse. Frank mounted his horse and gestured for the group to move out.

The hooves and the trundling of the buckboard's wheels seemed louder in the night air. Frank led the procession, riding his horse at a trot to produce the noise. Earl drove the buckboard, with Eddie sat beside him. Lester followed the buckboard, leading Earl's horse along the way.

Joe brought up the rear on his own horse. He looked over his shoulder as the lights in the town shrank into the distance. A wolf's howl echoed from Mount Elbert. Joe ignored it. He continued to watch the trail behind them. No other riders appeared. He kept following the group, watching the moonlight reflect off the ripples in the Arkansas River.

***

The sun rose over the Rocky Mountains as the procession reached Granite. Joe's eyes stung as he grew accustomed to the change in lighting. They came to a halt as they reached the hotel. The deputies who had driven the prison wagon left the jail and nodded to them.

"That's a relief," Frank said. "It looks like Crawley made it to the prison yesterday."

"And it doesn't look like they followed us," Joe dismounted and hitched his horse.

"You take care of Mr. Ballard," Frank said. "I'll see to Mr. Crawley."

"Is it safe to talk now?" Eddie asked.

"Yep," Joe helped him off the buckboard and handed him his cane. "Come on, let's get some breakfast."

Chapter 10
A Meal to Die For

Rain fell against the roof of the Granite Hotel as the sun set. Joe leaned on the porch with his cigar. The trail leading into town resembled the Arkansas River. Through periodic lightning flashes, he saw a group of four riders making their way up the trail.

Their horses' hooves splashed in the water. They pulled their hats low, preventing him from seeing their faces. Joe took a position behind the porch. He rested a hand on his Remington. The four riders didn't look his way.

They rode past the hotel without stopping. Joe watched them leave. He tossed his cigar into the crude stream and walked back inside.

In the foyer, the Labrador retriever Joe had seen during his previous visit trotted over to him. Joe stared at the dog, which sat down and wagged his tail.

"He must want to go out," The manager, a younger and better dressed man than the one in Leadville, peered up from his ledger at the front desk.

"It ain't the weather for going out," Joe knelt down and petted the dog.

"It really isn't," The manager said.

"What's his name?" Joe asked.

"Rufus," the manager replied. "Well, that's what I called him. Must have been a working dog that got abandoned. He wandered in here a few months back. I put up signs, but nobody came to claim him. So he just lives here now."

"Any other strangers arrive today?" Joe stood up.

"No, sir," the manager said. "To be honest, most people ride on towards Leadville."

"Right," Joe said.

"I take it you and your deputies will stay for dinner?" The manager asked.

"Yep," Joe nodded. "I'm gonna see if my friend's ready."

Joe walked upstairs to Eddie's room. The sound of harmonica music came from within. He paused for a moment to listen to the tune, recognizing it as "Red River Valley". He knocked on the door. The music stopped.

"Who is it?" Eddie asked.

"It's Joe," he replied. "Just wondering if you're ready for dinner."

"Sure," Eddie replied. "Come on in."

Joe stepped inside. Eddie sat at the room's desk. He placed the harmonica back in its tin case.

"I didn't know you played harmonica," Joe said.

"More like dabble," Eddie replied. "It's how I pass the time since I can't read or go out at the moment. Is it bothering you?"

"It's fine," Joe said. "I'll let you know if someone else complains."

***

Joe sipped his beer as he sat at the table in the private dining room with Eddie, along with Earl and Lester.

"This beer ain't bad," Eddie took a sip from his own glass. "And the breakfast here was much better than the ones in Leadville. If the dinner is just as good, maybe I should move here permanently."

"What was it you were doing before?" Earl asked Eddie. "What brought you to Leadville?"

"The promise of minerals, mainly," Eddie replied. "Used to be a prospector when I still had eyes that worked. Found a few decent pockets, but that ended up being my pension when I went blind."

"Yeah, I thought of going into the mining business too," Earl said. "But there are too many companies laying claims. I needed to make a bit of money, and I had a talent for getting folks to listen without pulling a gun, so I ended up becoming a lawman."

"Is there another fella sitting with you?" Eddie asked. "He's awful quiet if he is."

"Lester doesn't say much," Earl chuckled. "But he's good at backing me up when I can't talk folks down. We make a pretty good team."

The tap of a foot on the door prompted Joe to stand up.

"Is this the Buchanan party?" A woman outside asked. "I've got two plates of the roast lamb and two more on the way."

Joe opened the door. A young woman in an apron entered with the meals.

"Something smells real good," Eddie remarked as she brought the food to the table.

Rufus trotted behind the waitress and darted into the room.

"Rufus, get gone!" She snapped at the dog. "I've told you before about begging in front of the guests."

"It's alright," Earl smiled. "We can keep him in here if you like. That way, he doesn't bother the other guests."

"That would be much appreciated," The waitress said. "Enjoy your meals and don't treat him too much."

She left the room and closed the door behind her.

Joe saw Rufus looking up at him with a pleading look in his eyes.

"Alright," He cut a small piece from one of the lamb slices. "Just one though. Got it?"

He tossed the piece of meat to the dog, who caught it in his mouth. Rufus wagged his tail as he chewed the morsel.

"You surprise me, Joe," Eddie carved up his own lamb slices. "You ain't a fan of people, but you sound like you're fond of animals."

Joe opened his mouth to speak when Rufus gagged. He and the two deputies peered over.

The dog vomited on the carpeted floor and then slumped over. Joe walked over.

Rufus lay still. The dog wasn't breathing.

"What's happening?" Eddie moved the morsel on his fork towards his mouth.

"Don't eat that!" Joe stood up.

Eddie recoiled at the raised voice. His fork fell out of his hand and clattered on the plate.

"Looks like Crawley's boys found out where we are," Joe said. "You two, get Eddie back to his room. I'm gonna check the kitchen."

He opened the door. The waitress appeared in front of him. Joe drew his Remington. She gasped. The two plates she carried fell to the floor.

"Sorry," Joe un-cocked the gun. "You see anybody in the kitchen who shouldn't have been there?"

The waitress shook her head. She trembled. Joe looked around. The dining room was empty.

"What in heaven's name is going on?" The manager entered the dining room. "I heard some dropped plates. I want this mess cleaned up at once!"

He fell silent as he met Joe's gaze.

"Someone tried to poison us," Joe said. "I need to check the kitchen!"

"This way," the manager stammered.

He led Joe to the kitchen. The smell of roasting meat and boiling potatoes greeted them. A cook in a once-white apron turned to face them.

"No guests in the kitchen," He reached for a cleaver. "I caught one person in here already and chased him out."

"I got a complaint about the food," Joe tapped the badge on his lapel. "What did the fella look like?"

"He wore a mask," The cook put the cleaver down. "I figured he was a thief, but he ran away before I could confront him."

"Where did he run to?" Joe stared at him.

The cook pointed towards the back door. Joe gestured for the cook and the manager to get behind him. He drew his Remington and advanced on the door. Glass crunched beneath his feet so he lifted his boot. What remained of a broken bottle lay on the floor.

"Have you found something?" The manager piped up.

Joe knelt down to examine the bottle. The glass shards were coated in a residual powder. A label had stuck to his boot. He peeled it off. The writing had faded, but he made out an image of a rat, accompanied by a skull and crossed bones.

"You got a rat problem?" Joe asked.

"Yeah," The cook replied. "I use a special poison to kill them. I think I've got a bottle somewhere."

He opened a high cupboard and stared at an empty space.

"That's what the thief was looking for," Joe stood up and dipped his hands in a wash bin. He wiped the murky water on his pants. "You two stay put. The marshal will have questions."

Joe left the kitchen and returned to the dining room. Lester returned with his revolver in hand.

"Is Earl watching the room?" Joe asked.

Lester nodded.

"We'd better get the marshal," Joe said.

The front doors crashed open. Four masked men burst into the foyer and turned towards the dining room.

"Look out!" Joe flipped the table. He and Lester ducked behind it as the men opened fire. Powder smoke filled the room. Bullets smashed into the overturned table, showering Joe and Lester with splinters.

"Looks like we got 'em boss!" One man said.

Joe turned to Lester and placed a finger to his lips.

"Guess he wasn't so fast after all," another said. "Carlton, Wesley. Get upstairs. Give the blind bat and those two gossiping ladies what's coming to them. We'll keep watch down here."

"You hit?" Joe mouthed. Lester shook his head. Joe drew his Colt Army from his second holster. Lester drew his own revolver.

Two pairs of footsteps drew closer. Joe nodded.

"Now!"

He and Lester emerged from behind the table. They fired their shots. The two masked men fell to the floor.

"Get to the jail!" Joe barked at Lester. He glimpsed the other two men heading up the stairs.

"Hold it right there!" Earl shouted from upstairs. Another shot rang out, followed by a thud.

Joe ran to the staircase. One man fired at Joe from the top of the stairs. The bullet shattered a flower pot near the front door. Joe fired back. The man tumbled down the stairs. Joe leapt over the body as he bounded upstairs. He reached the hallway. Earl lay dead on the floor outside Eddie's room.

"Who's there?" He heard Eddie say in a frightened tone.

Joe raced towards the open bedroom door with his Colt drawn. The last man was inside. He had his arm around Eddie's neck and pointed a gun at his head. Joe inched inside, keeping his revolver trained on the killer.

"Stay back!" The masked man shouted. "Or the blind man dies!"

"Not the best plan," Joe said.

"Oh really?" The man gave a high-pitched laugh. "I'm real scared."

"You sound it," Joe replied. "You're cornered. The marshal would have heard the shooting at the jail. Let him go and give yourself up. You shoot him, and you'll leave the room in a pine box."

The man inched towards the window with his hostage.

"You don't want to risk his life," he said. "You need him alive to testify."

"And you need him alive if you want any hope of walking out," Joe stared him down. His eyes narrowed. Beads of sweat poured down the masked man's forehead and soaked into his bandana.

"Joe, please," Eddie whimpered. "I ain't ready to die."

"Neither's he," Joe said. He switched his Colt Army to his left hand.

"I'll take a chance," the masked man raised his gun at Joe.

Joe drew his Remington with his right hand and fired.

Eddie yelped.

Blood trickled down the masked man's face from beneath his hat. His eyes had widened as he fell back against the wall.

"You okay?" Joe holstered his guns and walked over to Eddie.

"I think I had an accident," Eddie stammered.

"You're fine," Joe said. "You still got that whiskey I gave you?"

"Yes," Eddie replied. "I think it's on the desk."

Joe picked up the bottle from the desk. He took a swig and handed it over to Eddie. Eddie took a long drink from the bottle like it was water.

The sound of footsteps ascending the stairs prompted Joe to draw his Remington. He spun round and aimed at the door.

"What the hell happened here?" Frank entered the room with his gun drawn.

"Crawley's boys found out where we are," Joe lowered his gun. "I think somebody's been talking."

"Dang it," Frank muttered. "You head downstairs and get yourself a drink, Joe. I'll handle this."

***

Joe sat in the darkest corner of the hotel dining room. Another bottle of whiskey sat on the table with a glass. The room was deserted. The hotel staff and other local shopkeepers had taken the bodies away and cleaned up the mess in the private dining room. He poured himself a glass of whiskey and nursed it.

Frank stepped into the dining room.

"Mind if I join you for a drink?" He asked.

Joe pointed to a vacant chair. Frank raised his index finger and stepped away. He walked over to the vacant bar and returned with an empty glass.

"Is Eddie okay?" Joe asked.

"He'll be fine," Frank replied. "He's sleeping off that whiskey you gave him to calm his nerves. When he wakes up, he will have clean clothes.

Joe nodded.

"I don't understand what happened," Frank sat down. "They didn't follow us so how did they find us?"

"Someone must have talked," Joe said. "Back in Leadville. If they knew where we were, they could have ridden out in the day."

"Do you suspect anybody?" Frank asked.

"A few folks," Joe said. "Maybe it's the sheriff. It could have been the hotel keeper or his wife. Or maybe it was Mr. Coffey or Miss Amy. I ought to head down to Leadville and find out who."

"In case you haven't noticed," Frank wagged his finger. "We're pretty short on manpower around here. I couldn't get many of my men from Denver. Most are elsewhere in the state. Why don't you take it from the beginning? Talk me through what happened tonight."

"It started when we were about to eat dinner," Joe poured the marshal a drink. "I gave some meat to the hotel dog, and he dropped dead. That's when I realized the food must have been poisoned. I went and checked the kitchen and the cook claimed somebody lit out."

"And he didn't check the meals he'd prepped?" Frank raised an eyebrow.

"He assumed that the man was a thief," Joe replied. "Do you want to bring him in?"

"I'll deal with him later," Frank raised a hand. "Then what happened?"

"They stormed the hotel," Joe said. "Four of them. Lester and me took care of them. But Earl didn't make it."

"I saw him in the hallway," Frank bowed his head. "Earl was a real affable deputy. Folks liked him. I don't think he ever drew a gun, but I hired him because of his ability to talk folks down."

"Talk don't seem to work very well in these parts," Joe took a sip of his whiskey.

"World's changing," Frank replied. "Eventually, things are gonna get less wild. What will you do then?"

Joe stared at the marshal.

"Well, it ain't what we're talking about now," Frank continued. "I'm glad Eddie's still breathing. What I ain't so glad about is that none of those boys are breathing anymore. We could have got them to give up Crawley or that Southern dandy of his."

"Crawley's in jail," Joe said. "He'd deny it. And I don't think anybody would want to give him up without looking over their shoulders for the rest of their days."

"That doesn't matter," Frank said. "If you have a chance to take someone in without killing them, take it. When you wear that badge, you're a lawman, not some hired killer."

"And if I don't have the chance?" Joe asked. "I was more concerned with keeping Eddie alive than questioning folks who weren't inclined to talk."

"Maybe you're right," Frank sighed. "But always remember that the badge comes before the gun."

Joe paused. He snapped his finger. "There was one thing, though."

"I'm listening," Frank leaned closer.

"I heard them barking orders to each other," Joe took another sip of whiskey. "They mentioned going upstairs after Eddie and the ladies."

"Which means?" Frank shrugged.

"They must have thought that Mrs. Hartley and her daughter are here as well," Joe said.

"If they tried to hit Eddie..." Frank stood up, "They might go after them as well."

He tightened his fists. "Where can we go?"

"I've got an idea," Joe said. "You should take Eddie to a new safe house if you can. Keep him moving. I should ride back to Leadville and find the ladies. That deputy we posted with them will have his hands full. I can figure out who's been talking to Crawley's boys while I'm there."

"Worry about the safety of the ladies," Frank interrupted. "I can't have my deputies getting suspicious. But great idea. I don't have enough men to guard Eddie around the clock. But I can keep moving him between safe houses while you find the Hartley ladies. I'll meet you in Leadville in three days."

Joe stood up.

"Get some rest," Frank said. "You leave in the morning."

Chapter 11
A Race against Time

The sky was overcast when Joe arrived in Leadville in the late morning. His horse panted as he walked through the tent city into the main street. He dismounted outside a livery stable on the corner.

"How can I help you, Deputy?" A stable hand walked outside.

"Make sure the horse gets some feed," Joe tossed him a coin. "I ain't gonna be in town long, but I want to make sure he's ready to ride."

He tossed him another coin.

"You got it, mister," The stable hand said with enthusiasm as he pocketed the second coin. He took the reins and led the horse into the stable.

Joe walked down the street towards the general store. As he approached, he heard sounds of breakage from within. Amy ran out of the store.

"Where the hell are you going?" A man chased after her, carrying an ax handle. She sidestepped and tripped him. The thug landed on the muddy street.

"Joe!" She said, "You gotta help us! My daddy's on the floor and those thugs are smashing the place up!"

"You'll pay for that, you damn..." The thug's voice trailed off as he met Joe's sharp glare. "Oh my ..."

The man scrambled to his feet and ran away from the store.

"Stay behind me," Joe said. "This could get messy."

"I'm coming with you," Amy picked up the discarded ax handle. "I'm sick of being pushed around by those scofflaws."

Joe stepped inside the store. Two more men were knocking items off the shelves with ax handles. Silas lay on the floor as a third man stood over him with his crutch.

"Who's gonna stop us now, soldier boy?" He said with a mocking tone. "You should have paid the dues when you had the chance."

"See if he feels anything in his bad leg!" The thug closest to the entrance cackled, his back turned to the door.

The man stood over Silas dropped the crutch as he noticed Joe enter the store.

"What is it?" The first man followed his friend's gaze and saw Joe standing behind him. "Oh..."

Joe floored the man with a haymaker. He fell against a broken shelf. Joe stepped over him and advanced on the other two. The second man tightened his grip on his ax handle.

"You leave him alone!" Amy barked.

"I thought you got killed in Granite!" The man who had held the crutch said.

"So, you knew about that," Joe's eyes narrowed.

The second thug swung the axe handle. Joe sidestepped. The man overbalanced. Joe elbowed him in the back of the head. He slumped to the ground.

"You'd better talk," Joe advanced on the last man. "Who told you we were in Granite?"

The thug pulled back the lapel on his jacket to reveal a gun in his holster.

"Be my guest," Joe said. "Tell me who leaked and you can limp out with your friends. But you touch that gun and you'll be leaving in a pine box."

"Fine," The man inched back and raised his hands. "It was old George at the hotel. He said his wife overheard you talking."

He looked over Joe's shoulder. "Stab him in the back!"

Joe heard wood breaking behind him. He turned. Amy stood over the first thug with the broken ax handle. The man lay unconscious, with a bowie knife clasped in his hand.

"Look out!" Amy yelled.

Joe turned back to the last man, who reached for his gun. Joe drew his Remington and fired. The man tumbled to the ground.

"I'm so glad you're okay," Amy cried to Joe and embraced him. "Those men were saying you and Mr. Ballard were killed in Granite."

"I almost was," Joe replied. "Come on, let's help your father."

They lifted Silas to his feet and helped him to the counter. Joe picked up the crutch and handed it to him.

"Thank you, Mr. Whitmore," He said. "Things have gotten worse these last couple of days. With you and the marshal being out of town and the sheriff nursing that head injury, there's not much in the way of law."

"I'll cart these rips off to the jail," Joe said. "Maybe they'll talk. But right now, I gotta pony up. Do you know where the Hartley family lives?"

"They have a ranch in the area," Amy replied. "It's a little out of the way, but not too far from the town. Why do you want to know?"

"They're in danger," Joe replied. "Crawley's men tried to poison us in Granite, then they raided the hotel. Killed a deputy while doing it. They might have tried to raid the ranch."

"That ranch is a hard place to sneak up on," Silas remarked. "They'll have seen anybody coming from miles away."

"Let's hope they held out," Joe replied. "Thanks for your help. I'd better get these two scumbags to jail before they wake up."

"I'll help you," Amy said. "But I can't ride with you because I gotta stay and look after Daddy."

"Don't worry about it," Joe said. "As long as there's a landmark, I should be able to find the way."

***

After locking the two thugs in the sheriff's office, Joe stared at the hotel. Townspeople crowded the street in response to the sound of the earlier gunshot.

"There's something I gotta ask about," he said. "You should head back to the store."

"You want to go after the hotel keepers?" Amy stammered. "Please, let it go. There's nothing to gain in revenge."

"I ain't looking for revenge," Joe said. "But I'm looking for answers."

"Well, I'm coming with you for that," Amy walked after him. "I don't want this getting messy."

Joe walked over to the hotel.

"It's okay, folks," He said to the townsfolk as he walked past. "There was some difficulty in the general store, but it's been taken care of. You can go about your business."

He ignored their stares as he entered the foyer.

George and Martha stood behind the reception desk and studied the ledger. Upon seeing him enter, they froze.

"Mr. Whitmore..." The hotel keeper stammered. "You're alive?"

"No thanks to you," Joe stared at the couple.

"Joe..." Amy nudged him.

Joe walked over to the front desk. He pulled both revolvers from his holster.

"Joe..." Amy said. "Please don't do this. What do you have to gain?"

"Take me," George moved his wife behind him. "I deserve this. But let my wife go."

Joe set the two revolvers on the desk in front of George. "If you want to kill me, this is your chance."

George remained still. He eyed the guns, but didn't move to take them.

"I'm not here to kill you," Joe took a step back away from the guns. "But I want to know why you did what you did."

"I..." George stammered.

"Just tell him, George," Martha said.

"Fine," George exhaled. "I've been paying protection money to Crawley's boys ever since I came here. But I can't afford to pay it all the time. Crawley's dandy came by and offered to accept payment in information if I couldn't pay in cash or minerals. He said to tell him about anybody who came to the hotel. Lot of gunmen wandered into town and he figured he could recruit them for Mr. Crawley."

"When did you tell Fate I went to Granite?" Joe asked.

"After you left," George replied. "He figured it would be easier than following you. I also lied and told him you'd taken the Hartley ladies with you to Granite. I knew Mr. Hartley when he was still alive and owed him that. Please don't kill me."

"I already said I won't kill you," Joe patted him on the shoulder as he went to recover his guns. "But I want you to do something for me. Next time Fate comes asking, you're gonna tell him I plan to take the Hartley ladies to Denver where they'll be in the care of the U.S. Marshals."

"What if Fate discovers I lied to him?" George fidgeted.

"He won't," Joe said. "If I know him, he's contracted to Mr. Crawley. But if Crawley hangs, that contract will be void and he'll have to find another job someplace else. And that's if we don't cross paths."

He tipped his hat and left the hotel. The onlookers had dispersed.

As Joe walked back towards the livery, Amy ran ahead of him.

"I'm glad you didn't kill them," she said. "Something tells me you wanted to."

"I've seen too much killing in my lifetime," Joe replied. "I hoped to make my way in some other line of work. I wanted things to be different."

"Why did you get into it at first?" She asked.

"Well, my folks had a farm in Kansas that got burned by border raiders from Missouri," Joe stared into the distance. "I was about seventeen years old and got away. One of them chased me but fell off his horse. I got his gun and shot him. It was the first time I ever killed somebody and felt real bad. But that fella was a murderer who'd killed my folks. And he had friends out there. I joined the army, and they were glad to have me. They put my unit in charge of defending Kansas from more border raiders. After the sacking in Lawrence, they ordered us into Missouri to seize farms from people with alleged sympathies. But those people weren't soldiers. It wasn't what I signed up for, so I cut and run. I kept drifting for all that time afterwards. Travelled all around. Kansas, Texas, Colorado. Even after the war ended, there were plenty of folks looking for gun hands. Folks just like Hudson Crawley."

Tears welled in Amy's eyes.

"I'm sorry you had to hear that," Joe said. "I've never really talked about this before."

"I did not know," Amy choked on her tears.

"Well, if you ever want to try your hand at being a clerk, my daddy could use another pair of hands," Amy said with a smile.

"I might take you up on that offer," Joe said. "But I got a duty to do first. Crawley must face justice. While I've never believed in law and order from the courts, I guess now's a good time to start. But I gotta get my horse. Hopefully he's been fed and watered and ready for the ride. How do I get to the Hartley spread?"

"Head west out of Leadville," she gestured. "Look for Turquoise Lake and follow that. They're on the tip."

As Joe led his horse out of the stable, Amy waited for him outside.

"Joe…" she said. "Will I see you again?"

"Maybe," He halted. "Maybe not. I go into every shootout thinking it's gonna be my last."

"But you're not looking for a shootout," she said.

"Nope," He replied. "So you're wondering if I'm gonna be staying in Leadville when my work here is finished? Probably not. If Crawley hangs, there might be plenty of folk who want to get even with me. I've found that everywhere I go. And I reckon the army still wants to go after me on account of my leaving before I was supposed to."

"Then I won't regret this," Amy stepped forwards and kissed him on the mouth. His eyes widened, but he relented and threw a free arm around her.

"I'll see you again soon," He stroked her chin before mounting his horse.

"Be careful," She replied with a smile.

Joe smiled as he loped out of the town. For the first time in a long while, he felt warmth in his heart.

Chapter 12
The Hartley Farm

The late afternoon sky was overcast as Joe's horse loped down a narrow trail towards the Hartley farm. Cattle drank at the edge of the lake, while the occasional prospector panned for gold on the opposite bank.

Ahead lay a small farmhouse, along with a barn and a corral. Joe looked around. They would see him coming from any direction. He slowed his horse to a trot, expecting somebody to come out and challenge him. Nobody emerged from the farmhouse. His heart beat quickened.

Reaching the yard, Joe tethered his horse to the corral fence. The yard remained quiet, except for the clucking of chickens from behind the house. He looked around.

Nobody else was in the yard. He noticed deep ruts next to the barn, as though a buckboard or wagon was normally kept there.

He walked over to the farmhouse and knocked on the door.

"Mrs. Hartley?" He called. No answer. "Mrs. Hartley? It's Deputy Marshal Joe Whitmore!"

Still no answer. He placed an ear to the door. He couldn't hear any sounds from inside.

"Hold it right there," A voice said, punctuated by the sound of a gun being cocked.

Joe looked behind. A man with a bushy tobacco-stained beard and a battered frontiersman hat pointed a shotgun at him.

"Where were you hiding, old timer?" Joe stood upright and raised his hands.

"Don't you 'old timer' me, sonny," The man said. "You got five seconds to state your business before I blow your head clean off."

"I'm looking for Mrs. Hartley and her daughter," Joe stared him down. "Are you one of her hired hands?

"I figured someone would come soon," He replied. "She said someone was coming after them on account of that gunfight in Leadville. She ain't here, and you're trespassing."

"Hold on a moment," Joe pulled back the lapel of his coat to reveal his deputy marshal's badge. "My name's Joe Whitmore. I'm a Deputy U.S. Marshal. I came to take Mrs. Hartley and her daughter into protective custody. If they ain't here, I need to know where they are. Their lives are at stake. And I'd prefer to be talking to someone who ain't pointing a gun at me."

The old man un-cocked the shotgun and propped it against the wall.

"That's better," Joe said. "Now, who are you and where can I find the Hartley ladies?"

"My name's Zeke," The man replied. "And you ain't the first fella to come by since they left."

Joe raised an eyebrow. "What did the other fella look like?"

"He had kind of a forgettable face," Zeke shrugged. "He said he was an old friend of the family. But I'm the oldest friend of the family and I ain't ever seen anybody who looked like him. Didn't even give me a name. I chased him away when I caught him poking around. Kinda like what I did with you."

"Did he have a badge, too?" Joe asked.

"No, sir," Zeke shook his head. "I didn't see no badge on him."

"Right," Joe said. "But you didn't answer my question. Where did they head off to?"

"Mrs. Hartley said she was taking her daughter away," Zeke scratched the back of his head. "Her cousin, Mr. Hennessey, has got a big ranch up north. She told the other marshal who's been staying with us she wanted to get away for spell. Things have been rough in town ever since that fire at the hotel. She felt she had to disappear for a while."

"Did the other deputy go with her?" Joe asked.

"Yes sir," Zeke nodded. "I reckon he's still with them. Hennessey's got a big spread and plenty of hands working on it. Most of them are former soldiers. If somebody means her harm, they're gonna be facing down an army."

"I need to take her back to Leadville," Joe produced a stogie and offered it to Zeke. "You know the way to the Hennessey Ranch?"

"Yes, sir," Zeke accepted the stogie.

"You got a spare horse?" Joe struck a match against the wall and lit the old man's cigar, followed by one of his own.

"Yes, I have," Zeke blew a cloud of tobacco smoke. "This ain't half bad. But I've heard there are some real good ones made in Havana."

"Get the horse saddled," Joe replied. "We're riding out."

As Joe returned to his horse, Zeke emerged from the barn. He led a scrawny-looking horse with him. Joe looked at the animal in disbelief.

"He may look like crow bait," Zeke grinned, bearing yellow teeth. "But this old nag served me well over the years."

"Right," Joe mounted his own horse. "Hopefully, mine can keep up."

Joe followed Zeke's horse out of the yard on a trail leading towards Galena Mountain. As they rode into a wooded area, the old ranch hand hummed, and then broke into an old song.

"Care to join me?" He looked back at Joe. "It'll keep the spirits up for the horses."

"I'll pass," Joe replied. He looked around.

"Suit yourself," Zeke smiled and returned to his singing.

As they rode deeper into the woods, Joe smelt wood smoke. He made a hushing sound at Zeke, who continued to sing.

"Quiet!" He hissed.

"What's your beef with my singing, son?" Zeke asked. "You ain't a music lover?"

"I don't hate music," Joe made darting glances around the trees. "But I don't want you singing right now. We ain't alone. Somebody's got a camp nearby."

"A lot of folks use these woods," Zeke said. "Hunters, loggers, foragers. A camp ain't out of the ordinary."

"What if somebody was watching the farm?" Joe asked. "We need to move quickly."

***

The sun was setting by the time Joe and Zeke emerged from the woods and arrived at the edge of the Hennessey Ranch. From his position on the hill, Joe noticed a much larger complex than the Hartley spread: A two-story farmhouse occupied the area, along with a large bunkhouse near the barn and corral.

Two riders approached them. Joe looked them over. Both wore thick chaps and bandanas. One had a battered derby hat. The other wore a black Stetson and carried a Winchester rifle in his saddle ring.

"This here is private property, gentlemen," The man in the derby said. "State your business."

"It's just me, fellas," Zeke raised a hand and walked his horse forwards. "I'm taking Mr. Whitmore to see the ladies staying with Mr. Hennessey. He's a lawman."

"What kind of lawman?" The man in the derby narrowed his eyes. His companion slid the rifle out of the saddle ring, but didn't train it on either of them.

"I'm Deputy U.S. Marshal Joe Whitmore," Joe pulled back his coat to reveal the badge on his shirt. "I'm here to take Mrs. Hartley and her daughter into protective custody."

"Alright," The man in the derby said. "You can follow us."

He turned his horse around and walked him forwards. Joe and Zeke followed. The second man lingered, taking a position behind the pair. He kept his rifle drawn.

Joe followed to the main yard. Other ranch hands were playing horseshoes or leading horses to and from the barn. They stared at Joe, who tipped his hat as he rode past. A man with a deputy's badge on his vest sat on a chair on the porch with a Winchester resting on his lap. Upon seeing Joe, he stood up and held the gun at the ready.

A large man with a white horseshoe mustache stepped out of the farmhouse. He wore a wide-brimmed hat and a brown jacket.

"Howdy, Zeke," He said. "What brings you out here? Who's the stranger?"

"I'm Deputy U.S. Marshal," Joe said. "I came for Mrs. Hartley and Miss Tina. And to reinforce Deputy Baldwin there."

Daisy Hartley emerged from the farmhouse.

"Mr. Whitmore?" She gaped. Realizing that she recognized him, the other deputy lowered his rifle, along with the trail hand who had escorted them.

"You know this fella?" the large man asked.

"Yes," Daisy said. "That's Joseph Whitmore. He works for Marshal Buchanan."

"Well, why don't you get off that horse and get yourself some coffee?" He said in a warmer tone. "Rusty, Lancaster, see to their horses. They must have been riding for days."

Joe nodded to the man in the derby as he dismounted. He and his friend lead the horses towards the barn.

"I'm glad you could make it," The large man gripped Joe's hand and shook it hard. "My name's Henry Hennessey, and this here's my spread. Sorry for the less than warm reception you had on the boundary, but somebody has been making threats against my cousin and her daughter. So we're a little wary of strangers on the ranch."

"Joseph Whitmore," Joe replied. "And I can't stay. I'm here to bring the ladies back to Leadville."

"We're allowed to leave?" Tina called from inside. She ran out onto the porch.

"Tina!" Daisy gave her daughter a stern look. "What did I tell you about running in Mr. Hennessey's house?"

"Sorry, ma," She replied. "I was just glad to see that Mr. Whitmore's still alive."

"Where did you travel from, Mr. Whitmore?" Henry asked.

"Granite," Joe said. "With a stopover in Leadville."

"Well, why don't you stay the night?" he replied. "Your horses could use a rest and I have space in the bunkhouse."

"I'd be much obliged," Zeke said with a grin.

Joe removed his boots and stepped inside the farmhouse. The interior was well-furnished. A large woman in an apron emerged from the kitchen.

"More guests for supper?" She said with a warm smile.

"This is my wife, Patricia," Henry said. "Darling, this is Joseph Whitmore. He's here to protect Daisy and Tina."

Joe removed his hat and nodded to her.

"Come on into the living room," she said. "I'll make you some coffee."

***

Joe sipped his coffee as he sat on a couch in Henry and Patricia's front room. A fire crackled away in the hearth, filling the room with the smell of wood smoke. Tina sat next to him while Daisy sat in a chair opposite.

"Is Mr. Ballard okay?" Tina asked.

Joe paused for a moment, and then nodded.

"Will we be staying with him?" She asked.

"Tina," Daisy raised a hand. "Spare Mr. Whitmore the questions. He's tired and needs to rest."

"It's alright," Joe said. "Marshal Buchanan is keeping Mr. Ballard on the move while we find a safe place to keep you."

"So, we're not staying at the hotel in Granite?" Daisy raised an eyebrow.

"No," Joe took another sip of coffee.

"Well, you're more than welcome to stay here," Henry said. "Mrs. Hartley has told me all about Hudson Crawley's trial. This place is pretty secure, and most of my hands came out here after mustering out."

"I still gotta get them back to Leadville for the trial," Joe said.

"How come we ain't staying in Granite, Mr. Whitmore?" Tina asked.

Joe said nothing. Daisy aimed another glare at her daughter. As she looked his way, he nodded. She nodded back in understanding.

Henry opened his mouth to speak when the sound of gunshots rang out in the distance.

"That's near the boundary!" He stood up and grabbed a shotgun hanging above the mantelpiece. "What the hell's going on?"

Joe followed Henry outside. He picked up his revolvers and cocked the Colt Army. Ike Baldwin stood with his Winchester at the ready.

"Somebody must be stampeding the herd!" A ranch hand ran to the barn. "Come on, we'd best round them up!"

"What's going on?" Tina peered out of the door.

"Stay inside," Henry said. "Could be rustlers, could be raiders."

"Assassins," Joe's eyes widened. "Keep everyone here! The stampede's a diversion!"

A dozen riders approached the yard. The thunder of hooves accompanied the sound of whooping and hollering.

"Get back inside!" Ike shouted. "They're heading..."

A shot cut his sentence off. He collapsed against the porch rail. More shots punched through the wood as Joe and Henry dove to the ground.

Joe scrambled for Ike's rifle. He picked it up and opened fire on the riders. Their horses bucked and whinnied. One man slid out of the saddle as a shot hit its mark.

The body disappeared under a cloud of dust. Some riders fired on the farmhouse. Others fired at the bunkhouse and the barn.

"How the hell did they find us?" Henry fired both barrels. A horse and rider fell skidded to the ground.

"They must have tracked me!" Joe fired Ike's Winchester. Another rider fell from his horse.

"Nice work!" Henry barked. He ducked as a stray bullet smashed a window behind him. "Never mind. Fight now. Talk later."

Shots rang out from both buildings. Joe glimpsed men in the windows, armed with repeaters or shotguns. Their barrage scattered the riders.

One man, thrown from his horse, scrambled to his feet. He raised his revolver. Joe fired back and dropped the man.

"Let's get the hell outta here!" someone yelled. The riders scattered and fled from the yard.

Trail hands emerged from the bunkhouse and fired at the raiders as they fled. One old hand fell as a stray bullet struck him. Joe watched the riders leaving. Another rider watched them in the distance.

"Fate…" he muttered.

As the shooting died down and the trail dust settled, an eerie silence filled the yard. Joe glimpsed at the bodies strewn across the yard. He looked over at them, along with Rusty and Lancaster.

"These fellas are real bold to be hitting the ranch like that," Rusty, the man in the derby, kicked a body over. "You recognize any of them, Lancaster?"

The man in the black Stetson shook his head.

"What about you, Deputy?" Rusty asked.

"Their faces ain't familiar," Joe said. "Probably hired from someplace else. Crawley's got a ranch and mines. He's got deep pockets to hire any fella who knows how to pull a trigger."

"I gotta admit," Rusty held his hat to his chest. "I never expected to be getting shot at again. Not since the war ended. Thought I might settle down and make it as a cattle rancher."

"War never ends for some," Joe said. "That's why I ended up drifting."

"Whereabouts have you drifted?" Rusty said.

"Around," Joe shrugged.

"Deputy," Henry tapped Joe on the shoulder. "I think we need to have a talk about what to do next. The rest of you, check on the herd. And keep your guard up. Those rips might be back."

***

Joe sat back in the front room and nursed a glass of whiskey. Daisy and Tina set opposite, trembling. Patricia Hennessey sat between them with her arms around both.

"Start from the beginning," Henry said. "What is going on here? I know that Mrs. Hartley told me what happened, but I want to hear your version of the events, too."

"Hudson Crawley and Fate Bullock tried to extort a local shopkeeper," Joe downed the whiskey in one gulp. "There was a gunfight and the shopkeeper and his boy got killed. Crawley executed the shopkeeper as he was bleeding out. Those two ladies saw the whole thing, and a blind fella named Eddie Ballard came forward saying that he'd recognized Crawley's voice."

"Was Crawley with the raiders?" Henry asked.

"I should hope not," Joe shook his head. "After Mr. Ballard told us what happened, Marshal Frank Buchanan and I served a warrant on Mr. Crawley. Last I heard, he's in the jailhouse in Granite."

"Could they have sprung him?" Tina's eyes widened.

Joe shrugged.

"Are you sure?" Henry leaned closer.

"Crawley offered to double the wages of anybody who'd help him beat the charges," Joe said. "If they sprang him, that'd only make him a fugitive. The deputies would seize his known properties so he couldn't go to ground there. No, he'd want to have his day in court. He'd want to go after the witnesses so they couldn't testify."

Daisy tensed up as he pointed to her.

"Have they made attempts before?" Henry folded his arms.

"Yes," Joe nodded. "For a while, it seemed like Mr. Ballard was the primary target, since his statement got him arrested in the first place. I got ambushed by two men in Leadville while taking him into protective custody.

Then that night someone cracked the sheriff over the head and tried to burn down the hotel. We moved him to Granite, then somebody tried to poison him.

When that didn't work, a band of four men tried to raid the hotel. They killed a deputy, but we fought them off."

"How come you didn't mention that when you arrived?" Daisy asked.

"I didn't want to worry anybody," Joe said. "But I guess we're way past that now."

"And where's Mr. Ballard?" Daisy asked.

"He went with Marshal Buchanan," Joe stood up and walked to the window. "We're keeping him on the move until we can get more deputies and find a safe house that can hold you all. That's why I came here."

"And you may have led them to us," Tina burst into tears. "When will this end? I thought we were safe here!"

"I'm sorry…" Joe stuttered. "I knew I was taking a big risk coming here, but I didn't think it would be that big a risk."

"That's happened now," Henry walked up beside Joe. "But I ain't gonna chew you out. You did what you felt you have to do. What I wanted to talk about was the next step. Where do we go from here?"

"They'll be back," Joe said. "And I need some air. I think we should see how many of your hands can weigh in."

Joe stepped out onto the porch and lit a cigar, watching the trail hands drag the dead gunmen away for burial. He offered a cigar to Henry, who declined.

"I'll double the watch tonight," Henry said. "Most of my boys saw action in the Civil War, so they ain't gonna fear some flannel mouth's private army."

"He'll have more men where they came from," Joe said. "If you're asking us to stick around, you gotta be ready for a siege. Will they be willing to stick around for that?"

"It's almost suppertime," Henry said. "We will gather the folks in the bunkhouse so I can talk to them there.

I can offer a little shooting money, but I can't force anybody to fight for me if they don't want to. I'm not one to take advantage of people's loyalties for my own ends for a thing like that."

Joe blew out a cloud of cigar smoke.

"Deputy?" Henry asked. "You know much about Crawley?"

"I've known plenty of bullies in my time," Joe said. "I can't see how Crawley's gonna be any different from them."

"Mr. Whitmore?" Daisy stepped onto the porch.

"You'd best stay inside and hunker down," Henry turned to her. "I don't think we're out of trouble just yet."

"I heard your conversation," She replied. "Tina and I have decided. We're going back to Leadville with Mr. Whitmore. If we stay here, I'm putting everybody's lives at risk."

"But what about Crawley?" Henry gaped.

"Mr. Crawley will be after us for as long as we're all breathing," She said. "But if my testimony can send him to the gallows, I'm certain it'll stop him from going after anybody else. Today has proven that nowhere is safe, so it's best that we stay on the move with Marshal Buchanan. Thank you for letting us stay here, and I'm sorry things ended up like this."

"None of this was your fault," Henry said. "You gotta do right by your daughter, and I'm gonna do right by y'all as much as I can. Cookie's gonna be calling us over real soon. We'll decide a plan then. But for now, I think Mr. Whitmore needs to eat and get some rest."

"I wouldn't say no to a hot meal," Joe remarked.

***

The interior of the bunkhouse smelled of sweat and tobacco smoke. A row of tables occupied the center of the room, while beds lined the walls.

Hennessey's ranch hands gathered on the tables as the cook gave them a helping of stew. Joe nodded to him and took a seat near the end of the table with Henry, along with Daisy and Tina.

"Are we all here?" Henry rapped the table. "As you all know, a band of raiders attacked the ranch today. Their intention was to kill these two ladies in my care."

He gestured to Daisy and Tina.

"Are you sure that's why they came here?" One ranch hand asked. "Why are they interested?"

"They're assassins," Joe didn't make eye contact with the other speaker as he ate a mouthful of the stew.

"Exactly," Henry continued. "Mrs. Hartley and her daughter here witnessed a gun battle and are planning to testify in court against the perpetrator, Hudson Crawley. I'm fairly certain y'all know about him."

Murmurs rippled down the tables. Henry gestured for silence.

"Deputy U.S. Marshal Joseph Whitmore is with us today," He pointed at Joe.

"He came to take them back to Leadville for the upcoming trial. Tomorrow is gonna be tough. We fended off one attack, but those rips are certain to try again. And there might be more of them. I'm gonna need double the normal watch tonight, both in the yard and around the herd. But this ain't your fight. If you don't want to take part in things to come, you're free to leave right now with any pay you're owed and no hard feelings."

He paused again. All the ranch hands kept their seats.

"I ain't running from a couple of hired guns," Rusty said. "I saw worse in the war."

Several ranch hands nodded in agreement.

"When are we leaving?" Tina asked, only for her mother to hush her.

"Tomorrow night," Joe said. "My horse needs to rest. I noticed one fella who hung back from the earlier shootout. I reckon that's Fate."

"Fate Bullock?" Rusty dropped his cutlery with a clatter. "Ain't he...?"

"Yes," Joe said. "He's a professional killer. And he's a former cavalry officer. Today's raid was likely to gauge what he's up against. He'll probably be ready for us if we leave in the day. It's better we slip away at night."

"We'll make it look like we're hunkering down," Henry said. "Getting ready for a siege. But we'll smuggle you out tomorrow night. For that, I'm gonna need a couple of volunteers."

"Count me in," Rusty said. Lancaster raised his hand.

"I'm with you too," A larger ranch hand stood up.

"Thank you, Amos," Henry said. "Now, I'm also gonna need someone to ride out tonight and try to get the word back to Frank Buchanan in Leadville."

"I can do that," A Native American stood up.

"I'm glad you could, Charlie," Henry turned to Joe. "Charlie was a scout for the army. He should be able to sneak past Crawley's boys if they try to surround the spread."

Joe nodded to him.

"I think that's settled," Henry sat down. "Now we just need to believe the Man Upstairs is on our side."

***

The overcast night sky bathed the yard in shadow. Joe walked with Henry and Charlie towards the barn.

"You'll need to get to Leadville and find Marshal Buchanan," Joe said. "Tell him that Joe Whitmore sent you. If he ain't in Leadville, find Silas Coffey in the general store. Give him the same message."

"Where can I find the marshal if he's not in Leadville?" Charlie fastened the saddle on his horse. "It'll be hard to pick up his trail if he's using the well-travelled routes."

"Granite's your best bet," Joe shook his hand. "Good luck."

Charlie nodded and walked his horse out of the barn. He loped out of the yard and disappeared into the night.

"He'll be fine," Henry said. "Navajo Charlie's the best man for the job. You'd best get some sleep. I can't have a good gun hand getting too sluggish. I'll talk to you in the morning."

He walked back to the farmhouse.

Joe stood for a moment and watched the horizon, before returning to the bunkhouse.

The interior was bathed in shadow. The off-duty trail hands lay in the beds, their snoring echoing through the room. Rusty, Lancaster, and Amos sat at one of the tables and stared at poker hands, illuminated by a single lamp.

"Hey, Joe," Rusty said. "Care to join us for a game?"

"I'd rather just sleep tonight thanks," Joe said.

Lancaster pointed to a vacant bunk. Joe nodded to him and walked over. He removed his boots, lay back on the straw-filled mattress, and closed his eyes.

Chapter 13
The Waiting Game

The creak of the door prompted Joe to open one eye as he lay in bed. The lamps inside the bunkhouse had been extinguished, leaving the interior in an almost pitch darkness.

He heard the door close. Whoever had just entered was trying not to make too much noise.

The other ranch hands continued to snore. The sounds of footsteps and creaking floorboards did little to rouse anybody.

Joe turned to the gun belt hanging from the bedframe. He wanted to grab the Remington, but something prevented him. He couldn't lift his arm.

A figure stood at the foot of his bed. Like at the hotel, his hat was pulled low and he wore a bandana that concealed his face. He drew a bowie knife from a sheath concealed beneath his coat.

"Say goodnight, killer," He said.

Joe breathed in. He could move his arm again.

"Mr. Whitmore?" A familiar voice asked.

Joe grabbed the Remington from his holster and aimed it at the masked killer.

"Whoa!" Rusty jumped back and stumbled against the table behind him.

"Don't shoot!" Amos yelled from nearby.

Joe looked around. The morning sun shone through the gaps in the bunkhouse windows. The commotion had woken up the other ranch hands. Some of them backed away.

Lancaster pointed his own gun at Joe.

"I'm sorry!" Rusty yelled. "I didn't mean to startle you!"

Joe blinked. Rusty was standing where the masked killer had stood. He un-cocked his gun, and then rotated the cylinder back to the empty chamber.

Rusty gestured to Lancaster, who lowered his gun.

"What was all that about?" Amos yelled.

"Take it easy," Rusty said to him before turning to Joe. "You were tossing and turning like a demon on a rack. Must have been having one hell of a bad dream. I just wanted to check you were okay."

"I get plenty of them," Joe returned his six-shooter to the holster. He sat on the bed and massaged his temples. "Have done since the war."

"You served in the army?" Rusty asked.

Joe nodded.

"Still having bad dreams about the war?"

"Something like that," Joe replied. He stood up and scratched himself. "I ain't never got peaceful sleep since before I joined the army."

"I'm the same," Rusty pulled up a chair and rested his arms on the back of it. "I was at Shiloh back in '62. Some days I still remember it like it was yesterday. I was filling my canteen from a nearby stream one morning, and the water was a shade of red. Tasted real funny too. That was a taste I never forgot. Where were you stationed?"

"Kansas," Joe lay back on the bed and turned away from Rusty.

"Well, I ain't gonna pry if you don't wanna talk about it," Rusty patted him on the shoulder. "Come on. The cook's making biscuits for breakfast."

Joe followed Rusty outside. He looked at the grey skies and ignored the aside glances from the other trail hands as they lined up for their breakfast.

The cook stood by a chuck wagon with a skillet, shifting dough in the oil with a pair of tongs. A pot of coffee brewed next to the fire. The smell of the frying doe and freshly brewed coffee made Joe's mouth water.

He filled a tin cup from the pot and took a biscuit the cook had made.

"Mr. Whitmore!" Henry strode over to him. "And Rusty, nice to you here too. I was wondering if I could talk to you. Amos and Lancaster as well."

The other two ranch hands walked over to him.

"You heard the earlier commotion?" Amos raised an eyebrow.

"Commotion?" Henry turned to him. "What commotion?"

"Just a bad dream," Joe said. "I get them sometimes and it can make me jumpy."

"One of them scars of battle you can't see," Rusty added.

"Indeed," Henry said. "But that wasn't why I had gathered you here."

"What's on your mind, boss?" Rusty asked. "What do you need us to take care of? Maybe Joe can help us?"

"Well, I've considered ranching as a different line of work," Joe said.

"That's what I wanted to talk to y'all about," Henry said. "I won't need your services today. Don't worry, you've earned your daily dollar already. Fact is, you're all taking a big risk tonight. With that in mind, I figured you deserve some loafing time. It's the least I can do."

Amos and Lancaster exchanged worried glances.

"Take advantage of it," Joe said. "I always figure most days are gonna be my last."

"That ain't something I thought I'd hear," Rusty shook Henry's hand. "Thanks for this, boss. Well, fellas, anybody for poker?"

"I'll join you in a minute," Joe said as the other three hands returned to the bunkhouse.

"You might as well enjoy the time as well," Henry gave him a friendly thump on the back. "Take your mind off things. I might even have some whiskey stashed somewhere."

"If I survive," Joe replied, "I'll buy the first round of drinks."

"Good luck, Joe," Henry shook his hand. "I'll talk to the ladies and make sure they're as relaxed as can be too. I'll send for you at sundown."

***

The bunkhouse was almost deserted as most of the ranch hands were out and about. Joe lay back on his bed and stared at the ceiling.

"Care to join us for some poker, Deputy?" Rusty called out.

Joe looked towards the table. Rusty stood at one end of the table and shuffled a deck of cards. Lancaster and Amos sat nearby.

"Sure," He walked over and sat beside Amos. "What's the ante?"

"No ante," Amos said. "We normally wager the chores. Maybe smokes."

Joe reached into his shirt pocket. Only one cigar left. He placed it at the center of the table. The others placed one cigar each and Rusty dealt out the cards.

"This is five-card draw, fellas," he said. "You can't discard more than three cards."

Joe leaned back in his chair and looked at his hand: Three tens, a five, and a nine. He looked around. Lancaster discarded three of his cards and replaced them. He remained stone-faced as he looked at his new hand.

"I got a question, Mr. Whitmore," Rusty discarded two of his cards and replaced them. "You mentioned that Fate Bullock was part of the raid yesterday. How did you know that? I didn't see him."

"I saw him watching from afar," Joe discarded the five and the nine. He drew an eight and a six. He shrugged and returned to his slouching posture. "He ain't the kind of fella to rush into a thing like that. I'm just wondering what his move is gonna be."

"You seem to know a lot about him," Amos discarded three of his cards.

"A fella tends to pick up these kind of things when they move in certain circles," Joe said. "But that's a life I'm trying to put behind."

"So, you're kinda like in his line of work?" Rusty asked. "A gun for hire?"

Joe nodded.

"That ain't the kinda life I'd want," Amos said. "I don't know why anyone would choose it."

"Because sometimes it's the only way to get by," Joe said. "It's a line of work that often leaves enemies. And if you settle down, they often find you."

Lancaster flipped his hand, revealing a pair of fives.

"So, you've travelled far?" Amos flipped his own hand to reveal a pair of queens, accompanied by a jack, a three, and a seven.

"You could say that," Joe said. "I probably know two hundred bartenders and faro dealers by their first names."

"I've heard that kind of talk before," Rusty flipped his hand to also reveal a pair of queens accompanied by a jack, but with an ace and a nine. "Sorry, Amos. Looks like I got the kicker on that one."

Joe said nothing. He revealed his three tens and scooped up the cigars in the middle of the table.

"What kinda talk is that?" Amos raised an eyebrow.

"That wandering gunslingers, good and bad, are on first-name terms with two hundred bartenders and faro dealers," Rusty scooped up the cards and handed the deck to Joe. "That they live in five hundred rented rooms and eat a thousand meals in cafes or hash houses. No home. No wife or kids. No prospects."

"Does herding cattle give you prospects?" Joe asked.

"Now that you think about it," Rusty stroked his chin. "No. It don't. But I prefer the open air of the ranch and the trail to the darkness of the mines. Prospecting never worked out for me. But I kinda like having a place I where I can bed down every night. Plus the grub ain't bad. Pay's peanuts though, but my army days made me hate the notion of getting paid to shoot folks. Still, I'd like to settle down with a nice girl. There just ain't many around here who ain't whores."

"That sounds about right," Joe shuffled the deck. "Well, I did have somebody. I tried to settle down with her. But I'd made an enemy and he tried to get even. She got caught in the crossfire."

"I'm real sorry to hear that," Rusty sat down and held his hat to his chest. "I won't say anymore if that's bothering you."

"Thanks," Joe placed a cigar on the table. "I'd rather just play cards."

The door to the bunkhouse swung open.

"Howdy fellas!" Zeke stepped inside with a bottle of whiskey. "I heard there might be a card game going on and was wondering if I could join?"

"Don't see why not," Joe said. "You got smokes are anything for an ante?"

"How about the winner gets a drink?" Zeke pulled up a chair and placed the whiskey bottle on the table.

"Go easy on that," Joe said. "We might be getting into some difficulty on the way back to Leadville."

"You drink?" Zeke asked.

"I drink," Joe said. "I just ain't drinking now. How are the ladies, Zeke?"

"Kinda nervous," Zeke said. "I don't blame them though. We all are. I heard plenty of stories about Fate Bullock. Likes to present himself as a gentleman or something."

"Don't believe that," Joe stood up. "I've met plenty of folks like him in my time. Beneath that dandy appearance he's likely utterly ruthless. I'm gonna step outside for a moment if you don't mind."

"Where are you off to?" Rusty said. "The cards are getting warm."

"I'm gonna have a chat with the ladies," Joe said. "See how they're doing. But I'll be back. It's been a while since I got into any card games since I arrived in this county."

"Hurry back now, ya hear?" Zeke said behind him as he left.

Joe stepped outside and walked over to the farmhouse. He stared into the distance. No riders approached the yard. Nobody was watching the ranch.

Henry sat by the porch and smoked a pipe.

"Morning, Joe," He waved him over. "You keeping yourself occupied?"

"Your boys and Zeke are playing cards in the bunkhouse," Joe said. "I was just gonna check up on the ladies."

"They're hiding inside," Henry said. "Ain't the kind of weather for it, but I don't want to bother them with my smoke. That's why I'm out here. Care to join me?"

"Sure," Joe sat in one of the vacant chairs. He pulled one of the cigars from his shirt pocket. Henry brought his pipe closer. Joe used the embers to light his cigar. He nodded and leaned back.

"Rusty said you had a bad dream earlier on," Henry said.

"Yeah, I spooked a couple of the hands," Joe replied. "Sorry about that. Did they complain?"

"Nah," Henry shook his head. "It ain't in their nature to complain. Besides, plenty of them still have bad dreams about the war. Was that you were dreaming about?"

"Something like that," Joe blew out a cloud of smoke. "Mr. Hennessey, I got a confession to make."

"I'm listening," Henry replied.

"I used to work for people like Hudson Crawley," Joe said. "That line of work leaves you with plenty of enemies on both sides of the law."

"So it ain't something you can settle down from?" Henry inhaled the smoke from his pipe.

"Not really," Joe shook his head. "Tried once. She was a lovely girl named Anna. Thought I could have started something new. Learned a trade in a town. Raised a family."

"What happened?" Henry asked.

"Somebody came looking to test their mettle," Joe stared into the distance. "I was out with her in Dodge City, so I refused. He tried to shoot me in the back. She took the hit. I gunned the man down right where I stood. But I didn't want the sheriff asking questions. So I had to leave. Couldn't even stay for the burial."

"Lord Almighty…" Henry gaped.

"Exactly," Joe looked back at him. "But I found somebody else in Leadville. Amy Coffey, who works in her pa's general store. She's real sweet. Almost like Anna in most ways. But I'm afraid she'll meet the same kind of death. I feel like…I ain't strong enough to go through that kind of loss again."

"Mister…" Henry stood up and patted him on the back. "I don't mind telling you this, but the future ain't written. It's up to you to change it. And if you don't right now, you never will. Take that step. Settle down with her. Don't worry about what the future brings. Just enjoy the time you got together, because nothing ever lasts. I know Miss Amy. She's a good catch."

"Thanks for the advice," Joe smiled. "Here's to hoping I'll be able to do that once this ordeal is over."

He stubbed out his cigar and removed his boots before stepping inside the house.

Joe looked into the drawing room, where Daisy and Tina sat on the couch in front of the coffee table. They both stared into the distance. Patricia stood in the hallway.

"They have said little lately," She said. "I guess they're worried about what could happen."

"I don't blame them," Joe said. "Is it okay if I talk to them?"

"Go right ahead," She beckoned for him to enter the room. "If you can, try to convince them to eat something. I made some biscuits earlier. They've gone cold, but they should still be fine. There's plenty left if you're feeling hungry."

"You might as well bring them through," He smiled.

Joe took a deep breath and stepped inside the drawing room. Daisy said nothing he walked through the door.

"Everything okay, ladies?" He asked.

"Joe!" Tina looked at him. "I didn't hear you come in."

"Sorry," Daisy added. "My thoughts distracted me."

"Penny for them?" Joe sat down.

"I'm just worried about tonight," Daisy said. "I've hardly slept since the raid yesterday. Too many things I'm thinking about. Like what if Charlie got caught? What if we get ambushed on the way back? What if Crawley beats the charges?"

"I understand your worries," Joe said. "I'm hoping Charlie got through. We would have heard shooting in the night if he'd been spotted."

"What if they ambushed him without shooting?" Tina fidgeted.

"I doubt that," Joe shook his head. "Crawley's boys seem like the trigger happy sort. Even with Fate reeling them in, somebody would have gotten a shot off before he could do that."

He leaned back on the couch. Daisy and Tina stared at him.

"Ladies," He leaned forward and clasped his hands together. "I ain't ashamed to admit this, but I'm scared too."

"You're afraid?" Tina raised an eyebrow. "You never come across as afraid."

"Some folks don't," Joe nodded. "We called it 'seeing the elephant' during the war. Never understood why. There comes a time when folks stop showing fear because they've seen too much of it. But fear's always gonna be there not matter how many time you've seen it. Even if you don't show that you're scared, it can haunt your dreams for the rest of your days. It's simply a matter of whether the fear controls you. Or you control the fear."

"Really?" Tina said.

"Yep," Joe nodded. "I'm gonna get you back to Leadville safely. And we're gonna make sure that Crawley swings before he does any more harm to anybody else. Then Mr. Littler and his boy can rest easy knowing that."

Tina nodded. A tear ran down her cheek.

"I heard you talking outside with Mr. Hennessey," She said. "About how you lost somebody you loved. I'll miss Pete dearly."

"I know you will," He held her hand. "But soon this ordeal will be over for both of us."

"What if Crawley beats the charges?" Daisy said. "Will he come after us?"

"He won't beat the charges," Joe said. "You and your daughter have the strongest evidence. The jury's gonna have a hard time doubting that."

Patricia entered the drawing room with a plate of cold biscuits.

"Am I interrupting anything?" she said.

"Nope," Joe replied.

"I figured the ladies might be hungry," She set the plate down on the coffee table.

"Actually, I'm starving," Tina picked up a biscuit. "I haven't had an appetite lately."

She bit into it.

Daisy picked a biscuit, chewing away.

"I'll be outside," Joe walked towards the door. "I'd get plenty of rest if you can. We're leaving at dusk."

Chapter 14
A Messenger Approaches

Frank said nothing as he rode down the trail with Lester in the late morning. Eddie followed close behind him, on a buggy driven by another deputy.

"How are you keeping, Mr. Ballard?" Frank asked.

Eddie let out a loud yawn.

"I get that," Frank said. "I guess it ain't easy for you to be up and about all the time. Once Crawley swings, you'll be back home safe and sound."

"Do you think Mr. Whitmore's okay?" Eddie asked.

"I hope so," Frank replied. "Joe's one of the toughest fellas I know."

"He's been through a lot, hasn't he?" Eddie asked.

"Yeah..." Frank said with a sigh. "He could never truly settle down after the war. There were things they asked us to do he couldn't stomach. Things we never talked about, but dreamed about plenty."

"I think I understand," Eddie replied. "I guess everyone has regrets and seeks comfort for them. Either in the Good Book or the Devil's drink."

"Killing's a troublesome business," Frank said. "It's a thing that stays with you for the rest of your days. Joe had a wife once."

"Oh, really?" Eddie raised an eyebrow. "He never mentioned that."

"I would have been surprised if he did," Frank replied. "They murdered her not long after they settled down in Dodge City. Some gunfighter with a grudge shot her in the middle of the street."

"That's awful," Eddie bowed his head. "I did not know."

"Like I said," Frank replied, "it ain't a thing Joe likes to talk about. You couldn't have known."

A rider approached them on the trail.

"Hold up," Frank gestured for the deputy, pulling the buggy to halt.

"What's happening?" Eddie asked.

"There's a rider approaching," Frank eased his Colt from his holster. The rider drew closer. He was a Native American dressed in trail clothes. "U.S. Marshals! State your business or keep clear!"

The rider halted.

"Are you Frank Buchanan?" He said with labored breathing as he raised his hands.

"Who wants to know?" Frank cocked the revolver. "You'd best be quick about it."

"My name's Charlie," The rider said. "I work for Mr. Hennessey, and I have a message from Joseph Whitmore."

Frank holstered his gun. "You can approach. But keep your hands where I can see them."

Charlie walked his horse towards the buggy. As he drew closer, Frank noticed his sweat-drenched shirt.

"You look like you've been riding for some time, friend," Frank offered him a canteen. "Now, start from the beginning. Who's Mr. Hennessey, and what's he got to do with Joe Whitmore?"

"I work on Mr. Hennessey's ranch," Charlie smiled as he took the canteen. He took a long drink and handed it back to Frank. "Two ladies have been staying there. Friends of his. Said something about a murder trial and threats. Mr. Whitmore arrived yesterday to collect them, but some men tried to raid us."

"Crawley's boys attacked the ranch?" Eddie said, prompting Frank to hush him.

"Yes," Charlie said. "But we fended them off. Mr. Whitmore says he will leave with the ladies tonight. They will meet you in Leadville in the morning."

"Then we'd best ride to Leadville," Frank said. "Charlie, are you willing to be deputized? Mr. Ballard here is also a witness in the trial, and I need all the help I can get to keep him safe."

"Of course," Charlie said. "I was a scout for the Army."

"Great," Frank said. "We'll head back to Leadville. Your horse is gonna need some rest."

Frank led the procession, with Charlie riding alongside.

"You said that the ladies were hiding on your employer's ranch," Frank said as they trotted along.

"Yes," Charlie said. "Mrs. Hartley and her daughter have been friends with Mr. Hennessey for a long time. They said they feared for their lives. Something about a Mr. Crawley going after them."

"Hudson Crawley," Frank replied. "Some mining magnate who wants to take over the town of Leadville. He might go after the ranches next."

"He had a lot of men," Charlie nodded. "There were almost a dozen riders who came into the yard and started shooting. They killed another deputy."

"But Joe and the other hands fended them off?" Frank asked.

"Most of Mr. Hennessey's hands were soldiers," Charlie replied. "They aren't scared by hired guns."

"That's good to know," Frank said. "But they ought to stay put."

"Joe was afraid of being besieged," Charlie said. "And the ladies were afraid that staying with Mr. Hennessey was putting his people's lives in danger."

By noon, the procession had returned to Leadville. Another tent city was visible on the opposite side of the Arkansas River, away from the town. From his position, Frank noticed that the new tents were less ramshackle than those in a typical miners' camp. An American Flag waved from one of the tents.

"Is that an army camp?" Frank said.

"Yes," Charlie replied. "They arrived yesterday. Patrolling the mines, or something."

A few townsfolk stared at the posse as they rode down the main street. They came to a halt outside the jail.

Frank scanned the crowd as he dismounted. Many of them returned to their businesses.

Amy Coffey ran out of the general store towards the jail as she noticed Charlie. Silas hobbled out behind her.

"You found him?" She said.

Charlie nodded.

"Good afternoon, Miss Coffey," Frank tipped his hat. "You've spoken to Charlie?"

"Yes," She said. "He came by this morning looking for you. Is Joe okay?"

"I haven't seen him since I left the ranch," Charlie replied. "But he should be here tomorrow."

"Come on," Frank said. "Let's talk inside."

He stepped into the jail with the other deputies and Eddie. The two men whom Joe had fought in the general store sat on the bench in the corner, shackled to the floor.

"Would anybody like some coffee?" Amy stepped inside after them.

"That would be much obliged," Frank replied. "You might as well sit in, Miss Amy. You got a stake in this matter as well."

She nodded and walked over to the stove.

"Crawley's boys haven't been around much lately," She said. "I was expecting them to try again."

One prisoner chuckled.

"Something funny to you, mister?" Frank glared at him.

"Most of Crawley's boys know where those gossiping harlots are hidden," He replied. "Fate's leading them to the farm as you speak."

"I know," Charlie said. "There's a few who won't be coming back."

The thug fell silent.

"Charlie," Frank said, "how many men did you see at the ranch?"

"A dozen rode in," Charlie replied. "Most of them rode out. I didn't see many when I left. But I reckoned they were on my trail, so I kept doubling back to throw them off. I evaded most of them."

"What do we do?" Amy asked. "I'm real worried about Joe."

"Miss Amy, would like to step outside for a moment, please?" Frank replied.

She nodded and left the jail. Frank scowled at the two prisoners and walked after her.

Outside, Amy leaned on the hitching post on the front porch and stared down the main street.

"I can tell that you're worried about Joe," Frank stood next to her. "Are you and he…?"

She nodded and gave a weak smile.

"I understand," Frank said. "But I don't have enough deputies to help him. I've got to protect Mr. Ballard in there as well. If we lose him, it'll hurt our case against Mr. Crawley."

"But so will losing the Hartley ladies," Amy said.

"I know," Frank massaged his forehead. "I'm sorry. Everybody else is afraid of Mr. Crawley…"

"Like George and Martha at the hotel," Amy interrupted. "I was with Joe when he confronted them."

"And they walked away from him with their lives?" Frank's eyes widened. "I don't know how you convinced Joe, but you're incredible. He's lucky to have you."

"Thanks…" Amy replied. Her voice was noncommittal.

"What was the deal with them, anyhow?" Frank asked.

"They were afraid of Crawley beating the charges," Amy said. "That he'd get even if they took a stand against him. I'm worried about daddy's store. But they'd think twice if Joe was around."

"Pardon me, Marshal," Silas stepped onto the porch. His crutch tapped against the wood.

"You heard all that?" Amy said.

"The walls ain't thick," Silas said. "But I've heard there's a cavalry company that's doing patrols in the area. Served a couple off-duty soldiers the other day."

"Yes," Frank grinned. "I think I saw their camp on the ride into town."

"I don't know," Silas shrugged. "I didn't ask."

"Well, it might be worth looking into," Frank replied. "I'll see that Charlie's horse gets fed and watered. Can you think of any place we can keep Mr. Ballard?"

"He can stay with us tonight," Silas said.

"It's just gonna be one night," Frank replied. "Once Joe's arrived with the Hartley ladies, we're gonna stay on the move until the trial. Much obliged for letting him stay though. Just be careful."

"Crawley's got it in for me already," Silas said. "I don't see how this is gonna change anything. Anyhow, I need to head back to the store."

He hobbled away.

"I should go too," Amy replied.

"That's fine," Frank said. "I'll keep you posted and bring Mr. Ballard over tonight."

***

Frank stroked his chin as he watched the sun set. He looked over at the saloon on the corner of the street. He stepped back inside the jail.

"Charlie, Lester," He said. "Keep an eye on things here. I'm gonna make some inquiries about raising some more men."

"Right," Charlie replied.

Frank walked over to the saloon. The sound of piano music grew louder as he approached. He stepped onto the porch. His boot contacted the layer of spilled whiskey and tobacco juices.

The door swung open. A man in trail clothes and a man in overalls tumbled outside. They exchanged profanity.

The ranch hand took a swing at the miner.

Frank cleared his throat. They both looked in his direction.

"Let me guess," Frank said. "Spilled drink, cheating at cards, or looking at you funny?"

The two men scrambled to their feet.

"You walk away right now, and I'll let it slide," Frank said. The two men nodded in agreement. "Now git!"

They fled down the street in opposite directions.

Frank stepped into the saloon. The smell of whiskey, cigar smoke, and sweat was overpowering.

Miners and ranch hands crowded the tables, laughing and joking. Saloon girls leaned over the mezzanine to entice potential customers.

Frank walked over to the bar.

"What'll it be, Marshal?" The bartender asked.

"I'll take a beer," He placed a nickel on the counter.

"Coming right up," The bartender replied.

Frank looked around the room. On one table, he noticed four soldiers in uniform, drunkenly singing along to the pianist's tune.

"We don't see many soldiers here," Frank said to the bartender.

"Yeah, they're on some kind of exercise," The bartender placed a beer on the counter. "Hey, they're paying customers. Business is business."

"Much obliged," Frank nodded and took the beer.

He weaved through the crowd of patrons, holding his breath as a drunkard lumbered nearby. He reached the table with the soldiers.

"Excuse me, fellas," he said.

The soldiers stared at him. Their eyes narrowed as they saw the holster on his belt and the badge on his lapel.

"Tarnation," One of them said. "Can't a fella get a moment to enjoy himself?"

"Relax," Frank said. "You ain't under arrest. I just got a few questions for you."

"Well, we ain't got anything to say," The soldier replied. "We're just letting off a little steam, then we're heading back to camp."

"Good," Frank said. "But I'd like to know who your commanding officer is. I need some men for a posse and I'm guessing you're gonna need authorization for a thing like that."

"It's Captain Benjamin Palmer who you want to speak to," The soldier replied. "We'll let him know you're coming."

"Much obliged," Frank tipped his hat. "How about I offer y'all a round of drinks for the info?"

The suspicion in the soldiers' faces dropped at the promise of free booze.

"Works for me," The soldier grinned.

Chapter 15
Ambush

Joe lay on the bed in the bunkhouse and stared at the ceiling again. Most of the ranch hands had bedded down for the night. The door opened. Amos stepped inside.

Joe stood up, fastening his gun belt and picking up the Winchester that he'd propped on the wall next to his bed.

Amos walked over to him. "The wagon's prepped, and the horses are saddled and ready."

"It's time," Joe replied. "Get the others."

He stepped outside. The night was cloudless and a full moon was out. A covered wagon stood outside. A wrangler stood with three horses, including Joe's.

Joe walked over to the farmhouse and knocked on the door. He waited. Henry opened it, nodded, and stepped away.

Daisy and Tina stepped onto the porch with their leather suitcases.

"Are you ready?" Joe asked. They both nodded.

He led them to the porch. Amos emerged from the bunkhouse with Rusty and Lancaster, along with Zeke. Lancaster carried his Winchester.

Zeke sat on the wagon and cradled his shotgun. Nobody said anything.

"Right," Joe said. "Who knows the way to Leadville?"

"I do," Rusty stepped forward.

"Then you'll ride point," Joe said. "I'm gonna bring up the rear in case someone tries to attack from behind. Lancaster, you stay with the wagon. Amos will take the reins and Zeke will ride shotgun. You want to keep them covered."

"What should we do?" Daisy asked.

"I need you to stay in the wagon and keep your heads down," Joe said. "If we have to stop, get down under it. You'll be less likely to get hurt that way. Stay there until the shooting stops. If I'm still breathing, I'll come for you."

She nodded in agreement. Joe signaled Zeke and Amos to join him. They dismounted the wagon and stood next to him.

"If anybody's keeping watch, they might not see much in the dark, but they'll hear a lot better," Joe said once everybody had gathered together.

"That means I don't want you making any more noise than needed. That means no talking, no singing, and everyone keep together. I take it you know hand signals?"

The trail hands nodded.

"Good," Joe said. "Let's mount up."

"Good luck, everyone," Henry said. "Y'all come back now, you hear?"

"So long, Mr. Hennessey," Joe shook his hand. "Thanks for all you've done."

"It's the least I could do," Henry replied. "You make sure those ladies get back safely. They're like family to me and Patricia."

"I'll do my best," Joe secured his Winchester in a saddle ring and mounted his horse. He walked the steed towards the trail and waved the procession on. As the wagon passed, he trotted behind it while looking over both shoulders.

***

The night sky remained clear as the procession reached a narrow gully. The trundling of the wagon seemed louder in the poor light.

Joe kept glancing behind him, and now made glances at the rocks and brush lining the top of the gully. An ideal place for an ambush, he thought.

The wagon bumped and banged as it rolled through the gully. The cacophony made Joe grind his teeth as it echoed through the sky.

There was a sudden crash. Yells from inside the wagon. Lancaster's horse reared.

"What the hell…?" Zeke yelled. "Get a lantern! Pronto!"

"Will you be quiet?" Amos hissed. "We've already woken the dead with that ruckus. Let's not lead them to us."

Joe trotted forwards. In the glow of Amos' lantern, he noticed the wagon at an angle. One of the front wheels had gotten stuck in a patch of mud.

"What's the hold-up?" Rusty asked as he approached. "I heard a crash and saw the light."

"Wagon's stuck," Joe said. "Come on. We gotta get it out. We're sitting ducks in this gully."

He dismounted and grabbed the Winchester from his saddle ring. He walked over to the wagon.

Zeke climbed down from the seat and grabbed a shovel hanging from the side. He stooped down and dug.

Joe heard his own heart beating, overlapping with the scrape of the shovel.

"Perhaps we should have gone a different way," Tina said as they clambered down, prompting her mother to hush her.

"Just stay calm," Joe said. "We'll be moving again real soon."

"I'll try to lead the team out," Daisy walked towards the horses, pulling the wagon.

"I need you to stay with the wagon," Joe shook his head. "Out there, you'll be in the open."

"Do you know how to get a wagon out?" Daisy folded her arms.

"Not really," Joe replied.

"I've been working on a farm all my life," Daisy said. "I figured I should make myself useful. And if I don't make it, then Tina can still testify in court."

"Fine," Joe said. "Lancaster, cover her. Keep your eyes open. Amos, you think you and Zeke can push the wagon out?"

"I can try, Deputy," Amos rubbed his hands. "But I'm gonna need help to do that."

"Lancaster and I will keep watch," Joe said. "Let us know when you're ready for a hand. If anyone's watching, this would be the best time and place for them to hit us. Rusty, give them a hand."

"Right, Marshal," Rusty dismounted and took a position behind the wagon.

"Can I do something, Mr. Whitmore?" Tina stepped forward.

"How are you with horses?" Joe asked. "Can you wrangle?"

"Sure," She replied.

"Keep hold of everyone's horses," Joe said. "Make sure they don't bolt if something happens. The last thing we want is to lose a horse."

"I can keep them together," Tina smiled as Joe handed her the reins of his horse.

The sound of metal on wood resounded as Zeke tapped the shovel against the side of the wagon. The echo made Joe wince.

"I've dug out the mud around the wheels," He slung the shovel over his shoulder. "Let's get the wagon out."

"Okay, let's get to it," Rusty leaned against the back, next to Amos. "Ready?"

Amos nodded.

"Push!"

The wagon remained stuck. Joe looked behind on the trail. He listened for any movement in the brush. Nothing.

"Push!" Rusty said again, with a strained voice.

"It ain't moving.

He pressed his full body weight against the wagon. There was a creaking as the wagon resisted. A rumble. The wagon lurched forwards.

"It's clear!" Zeke yelled.

"Right," Joe leapt up and grabbed the Winchester before it moved away. "Everyone back to their positions. Quickly. I don't want to be out here longer than we have to."

He remounted his horse. Amos and Zeke helped Daisy and Tina back into the wagon before returning to the driver's seat. Rusty and Lancaster walked their horses back to the position.

As Rusty rode ahead, the wagon rolled forward.

"Now we're moving again!" Zeke said with glee, only for Amos to hush him.

The wagon followed the gully around. As it cleared the turn, gunshots rang out. The horses whinnied. Amos yelled as he yanked the reins. The wagon ground to a halt, and Zeke fell from the seat.

"Zeke!" Tina screamed.

Joe spurred his horse forwards.

"Zeke's bleeding!" Tina jabbered as she scrambled out of the back of the wagon.

"Get underneath the wagon!" Joe helped her out. "Amos, release the team."

"But we'll be stuck if they run away!" Amos yelled back.

"Do it!" Joe glared at him. "There's no room to turn around. We have to make a stand!"

Lancaster's horse bucked and reared, throwing the rider to the ground. Joe heard horses running away from them between the gunshots.

He dismounted and crouched behind the wheel. Daisy and Tina lay beneath the wagon. The wagon's team bolted as he released them from the yoke.

"Great, now we can't run away," Amos drew a revolver and fired. "We should have stayed on the ranch."

Joe glimpsed the brush ahead of the gully. Another shot rang out. He glimpsed the muzzle flash and fired a shot back. More shots retorted.

He ducked back behind the wagon.

Lancaster limped over to his position and pressed against the side of the wagon with his Winchester. He gave an audible wince as he took cover.

"You hit?" Joe asked.

"Leg's busted," Lancaster replied. "From getting thrown."

"Cover me," Joe said. "I'm gonna check on Zeke."

Lancaster nodded. He fired off three shots towards the brush.

Joe shuffled over to Zeke, who lay face-down in the dirt. He grabbed his shoulder. Zeke lay still. Joe rolled him over and squinted. He remained motionless. Joe shut his eyes and grabbed the discarded shotgun. He shuffled back to the wagon.

"They'll have seen our horses bolt," Rusty joined them, his revolver in hand. "They must be hiding in the brush. Counted at least ten shots."

"Then they'll be coming," Joe peered beneath the wagon. Daisy lay atop of her whimpering daughter to shield her.

"You'd better take this," Joe handed her the shotgun.

"I've never shot a man before," Daisy's arms trembled as she took the gun. "Don't you want it?"

"It's no good," Joe said. "They're too far away. Keep it until they get close."

Daisy nodded.

"Here they come!" Rusty hissed as he tapped Joe on the shoulder.

Joe looked ahead and made out the shadows of a group of men clambering into the gully.

"Wait," he said. Rusty and Lancaster nodded.

The men drew closer as they entered the gully. Someone gave a sadistic cackle which carried on the wind. Joe breathed in, then exhaled.

"Now!" He emerged from behind the wagon and fired on them. The three trail hands opened fire as well. Some of the shadows dropped to the floor.

Others scattered and tried to return fire. In the muzzle flashes, Joe glimpsed faces concealed behind masks. They began to flee back towards the brush.

"Let's get them!" Rusty emerged from behind their cover, firing his revolver.

"Wait!" Joe snapped.

More muzzles flashed from above the gully. Rusty yelled as he fell to the ground.

Joe handed his repeater to Amos. He ran out and pulled Rusty back towards the wagon. Bullets chipped away at the ground near his feet.

"I'm fine," Rusty said as they were behind cover. "Just the shoulder."

Joe took his rifle back from Amos. He squinted at a shadow in the brush in the rifle's sights and pulled the trigger.

The gun clicked. He pulled the lever. No round ejected.

"Out of ammo," Amos said.

"They ain't retreating," Joe sat back. "There's still some in the gullies."

"What do we do?" Daisy asked.

"We stay put," Joe said. "I think they're gonna try to wait us out. They'll probably try again in the morning."

"Nice work, general," Amos said. "We don't have any food or water for that kind of time. They could attack again any minute."

"So we wait," Joe said. "If you want to surrender, go right ahead."

"That'll be the day," Amos folded his arms.

"We probably took out a few of them," Joe said. "They ain't gonna risk that again. They might have thought we'd try to make a break for it."

"But we can't," Amos said.

"No," Joe replied. "So we wait."

Chapter 16
Behind Schedule

Frank leaned against the wall of the prison and watched the main street. He checked his pocket watch.

"Charlie," he stuck his head through the doorway. "Can you come out here, please?"

Charlie stepped onto the porch. "What is it, Marshal?"

"How long would it take to from the Hennessey Ranch to Leadville?" He asked.

"Usually around three hours," Charlie replied. "It took me longer, travelling at night and throwing off anybody trying to track me. But they should have arrived by dawn. That's when I arrived here."

"Something's happened," Frank snapped his watch shut. "I'll need you to show me the way to the Hennessey Ranch."

"I can do that," Charlie nodded. "But we don't have many men."

"Not deputies," Frank said. "But I have a plan."

He stepped inside the prison. Lester sat with his feet crossed on the desk.

"Lester," he said, "You stay and keep watch on Mr. Ballard. Charlie and me are gonna look for Joe."

Lester nodded in agreement.

As Frank stepped outside, Charlie stared at him.

"Come, on," Frank said. "Let's go."

"How are the two of us going to save Joe from Crawley's gunmen?" Charlie asked, "There were at least a dozen who raided the farm and Lord knows how many more he's got."

"I said I have an idea," Frank winked. "We're gonna show up with the cavalry."

***

Frank and Charlie led their horses to the new encampment. A length of barbed wire enclosed the boundaries of the camp, save for an entry point on the trail.

Two soldiers stood guard at the entrance to the camp, with Springfield carbines over their shoulders.

"Halt!" He raised a hand as the two men approached. "State your business!"

"I'm U.S. Marshal Frank Buchanan," Frank displayed the badge on his lapel. "I'm here to speak with Captain Palmer."

"Ain't he the fellow who spoke to those boys in the saloon last night?" The second soldier muttered near the first.

"You find the captain," The first one said. "I'll wait here."

The second man nodded and walked into the camp.

Frank looked at his watch. The young soldier who remained stared at him.

"How long do you think the captain's gonna be?" The marshal asked. "We're in something of a hurry."

The soldier shrugged.

"Been with the army long?" Frank asked.

"Fresh outta training," The soldier replied. "Wanted to serve the country."

"Well, shooting folk ain't a way to make a living," Frank replied. "Kid, you're gonna be in for a tough ride whether you're pitted against Indians or somebody else."

The second soldier returned to the gate with another man.

"Captain Palmer will see you," he said. "Follow me."

He gestured for his comrade to take the horses.

Frank followed the soldier through the camp. Soldiers sat outside their tents polishing weapons or playing five-finger-fillet on camp tables.

They reached a larger tent in the center of the camp. Another man stood guard outside. Upon seeing them, he pulled the tent flap aside. Frank nodded to him as he entered.

The interior of the tent was almost like a hotel room. Besides the cot was a privacy screen and a liquor cabinet, along with a large table strewn with maps and orders.

A well-groomed man dressed in an officer's uniform stood over the maps.

"Sir!" the escort saluted him. "U.S. Marshal Buchanan to see you, sir."

"Thank you, soldier," The officer returned the salute. "Leave us."

Frank watched the soldier leave.

"U.S. Marshal Buchanan?" The officer walked over and extended his hand. "I'm Captain Benjamin Palmer. I understand you talked to some of my men in the saloon last night?"

"Yes," Frank replied. "I've come to request some help."

"Care for a drink?" Palmer walked over to the liquor cabinet. He produced a bottle of whiskey and two glasses.

"No thanks," Frank raised a hand. "I'm in kind of a hurry. See, one of my deputies is escorting two witnesses in an upcoming murder trial and has failed to arrive. Charlie here is a hired hand at the ranch they were staying at and told us that some men tried to raid them the other day. I'd like to deputize some of your men to find him."

"I don't know if I can spare the men," Palmer said. "I won't be in this area too long. We're getting shipped to Wyoming to deal with some Sioux on the warpath."

"These boys are green, aren't they?" Frank asked. "Might be some chance for them to see some action for the first time."

Palmer froze. "Who's the fella on trial?"

"Some big mining magnate named Hudson Crawley," Frank replied. "He's been shaking down shopkeepers in Leadville, and he killed a man and his boy for trying to resist. The man's got deep pockets, and has been hiring guns to do his dirty work."

Palmer stroked his chin.

"Captain, I hate to hurry you," Frank said. "But we're short on time. My deputy and two innocent ladies could lose their lives if we don't act right away. I've got another witness who has faced similar attempts on his life since he came forward."

"When did he set out?" Palmer asked.

"Last night," Charlie said.

"What's the government's funding like?" Frank asked.

"What do you mean by that?" Palmer raised an eyebrow.

"Crawley gets found guilty, the federal government will seize his assets," Frank leaned on the table. "Might even be a bonus in it for your company."

Palmer gave an approving nod.

"Very well," he said. "Will you follow me?"

Frank stepped outside the tent. A burly looking sergeant with a scar on his cheek walked past.

"Sergeant Rothwell!" Palmer barked.

"Sir!" The sergeant stood at attention.

"Get ten men ready to ride out by the camp entrance," Palmer said. "The marshal here's forming a posse."

"Yes sir!" The sergeant saluted. Palmer returned the salute.

"Thanks, captain," Frank shook the officer's hand.

"Let's find your man."

Chapter 17
Under Siege

Joe yawned as he lay back against the wagon. He saw the gunmen moving across the top of the gully. His stomach rumbled. Buzzards circled the area.

Lancaster sat against the wheel, with Joe's empty Winchester strapped to his leg as a makeshift splint. Rusty sat beside him, his shoulder wrapped in bandages made from the wagon's canvas. Daisy and Tina continued to hide beneath the wagon. Tina whimpered as Daisy tried to hush her.

"It's almost noon," Rusty said. "Why haven't they attacked?"

"Someone's coming!" Amos yelled.

Joe picked up Lancaster's repeater and stared down the sights. Five riders trotted into the gully. The lead rider waved a white cloth. As they drew closer, Joe noticed the man had an immaculate appearance in his fancy white suit.

"Mr. Whitmore!" The lead rider yelled out in a familiar articulate Southern accent.

"Ain't that...?" Rusty said.

"Fate," Joe nodded. He inched upwards, keeping the rifle trained on the messenger.

"I know you're there, Mr. Whitmore," Fate continued. "I've come to talk."

"I gathered!" Joe yelled back. "If you've come to surrender, that's fine by me."

"You still think you can fight your way out of this?" Fate said. "I've been watching this gully for most of the night. Most of those boys wanted to hit you while you were getting the wagon out. But I reeled them in. I figured you'd be less alert if you were moving again. I planned to starve you out, but some of my men were impulsive and paid the price. Others wanted to sneak in and slit your throats during the night. You've cost Mr. Crawley a lot of men. And I respect that. So I've come with a proposition: Hand over the two ladies and I'll let you walk away."

"Don't even think about it!" Daisy snarled. Joe hushed her.

"You know I can't do that," He called back. "They know you're here to kill them."

"I don't kill women," Fate replied. "But you do!"

"What?" Tina mouthed.

"Is that a fact?" Amos called out.

"That's a fact," Fate replied. "He didn't tell you? I don't blame him. War takes you to dark places sometimes. His unit occupied Missouri. Seized farms from good honest folk on the grounds they were suspected guerillas. They executed those who resisted without trial. They weren't soldiers. They were simple folk trying to work the lands. And they say the South was in the wrong."

"I don't believe it," Tears welled in Tina's eyes. "I thought you were one of the good guys."

"There are no good guys with guns," Joe said. "Those were our orders. My unit carried them out. But I didn't. I'm wanted for desertion. Damned if I do. Damned if I don't."

"I'm waiting for your answer!" Fate called out. "Bring those ladies out here!"

"How about I call you out?" Joe yelled back. "I'll see just you with an iron."

"Don't do it!" Daisy hissed. "It's an ambush. He did the same thing to Mr. Littler."

"We're already in an ambush," Joe handed the Winchester to Amos. "I'm heading out. Keep me covered."

Joe stepped out into the open. He noticed the bodies of the men killed in the night attack. Nobody seemed to be on top of the gully. Fate handed his reins to one of his men and dismounted. He strode forward.

"I asked you to bring out the ladies," Fate said. "What is this?"

"You're the gentleman," Joe spat on the ground. "You figure it out."

"You seek an affair of honor?" Fate grinned.

"If it'll shut you up," Joe said. "That voice of yours is real grating."

One of Fate's henchmen chuckled at the remark. Fate looked over to the man, who fell silent.

"Very well," he said to Joe. "I accept. This will be like putting down a rabid dog."

A silence fell across the gully, save for the wind and the nickering of the horses. Joe's eyes narrowed as he stared Fate down.

"Is this going to be your last action on this earth?" Fate sneered. "Taking a bullet for those ladies? I respect that, but it will be for nothing."

"Draw," Joe said. His Remington left his holster and barked. Fate drew his own six shooter. The two shots echoed through the gully. Fate's shot punched into Joe's upper arm. He fell to the ground.

"Mr. Whitmore!" Daisy screamed.

"Let's get them, boss!" One of Fate's men said.

"Wait," Fate replied through gritted teeth. "I'll finish this first."

Joe peered upwards. Fate lumbered towards him. He noticed a red patch on his white suit. As Fate drew closer, Joe cocked his Remington. Fate stood and raised his Schofield.

"Was that suit new?" Joe forced a smile. "You don't look too good."

"It looks like I won't make it back to town," Fate said. "And neither will you."

Another shot rang out. A hail of buckshot knocked the white-suited gunslinger off his feet. Horses whinnied. Joe looked back. Daisy peered out from beneath the wagon with the smoking shotgun. He exchanged a nod with her.

Joe stood up and wobbled, but maintained his hold on the Remington.

Fate's men struggled to control their rearing horses. One bolted away. Another rider drew a revolver and aimed it at Joe.

"It's your call," He squinted at the three men. "What good's a bonus when you're dead?"

The sound of a bugle prompted the riders to look towards the gully's opening.

"Is that the cavalry?" Amos said from behind the wagon.

The three riders followed their companion out of the gully.

"Halt, or we'll shoot!" A commanding voice said.

Joe noticed a group of riders enter the gulley and cut off the retreating henchmen, who raised their hands. He counted a dozen men in blue uniforms. One of them rode towards him, along with two men in trail clothes. He recognized Frank and Charlie.

"Joe!" Frank piped up. "Thank the Almighty you're still breathing."

He dismounted and shook Joe's hand.

"Glad you could make it," Joe replied. "I took a bullet, but it looks like it went clean through. I guess Fate and his boys expected us to leave."

"Where is Fate anyhow?" Frank asked.

"Met his namesake," Joe pointed to Fate's body. He walked over and kicked dust atop the corpse to show his respect. "I see you got the men you needed."

"You're right," Frank showed the officer, who dismounted and approached. "Captain, this is Joe Whitmore, my deputy."

"Glad you're still alive," Palmer shook Joe's hand. "Say, aren't you Corporal Joseph Whitmore from the 1st Kansas Infantry? I heard there was an arrest warrant for a man of that name. Desertion."

"War ended twelve years ago," Joe replied. "Surely we're past the statute of limitations on that?"

"That was not the question I asked," Palmer gripped the hilt of the saber on his belt. "Did you serve in the 1st Kansas Infantry?"

"No," Joe's eyes narrowed. "You must have me confused with someone else."

"Captain," Frank stepped forward. "I can vouch for this man's identity. The Joseph Whitmore you're thinking of died in Mexico about seven years back. At least, that's what I heard."

Palmer looked back at Frank.

"Captain," Daisy stepped out with Tina. "I can also vouch for this man's identity. He's no deserter, and he saved our lives. He doesn't deserve to be treated like a criminal."

"Very well," Palmer said. "We should get your men some treatment and find a safe house for the ladies."

"That'd be much obliged," Joe said. "And I could use a drink."

Chapter 18
The Trial

Two days passed. Joe sat in the dining room of the Leadville Hotel, which had been rearranged into a makeshift courtroom. Daisy and Tina sat at his table, along with Eddie and Carrington.

Silas and Amy sat behind them. Joe exchanged a smile with Amy. He noticed Tina fidgeting while Daisy rested a hand on hers.

Crawley sat at another table, guarded by two deputies. A lawyer sat next to him, looking over a set of papers. He glowered at Joe.

"Well," Carrington said. "Today's the day. And the testimony from those men the army captured will add to the charges."

"You recognize the lawyer?" Joe asked.

"Mr. Gregory," Carrington replied. "He's a man who likes to win, so we'd best be careful."

"Surely this is an open and shut case?" Eddie replied.

"You never know," Carrington stroked his chin.

"All rise for Circuit Judge Clyde Panghorn," Frank said.

Joe stood up as the judge took his seat.

"Please be seated," He said. "Hudson Crawley, you are charged with the murder of Malcolm and Peter Littler, extortion, and conspiring to murder Eddie Ballard, Daisy Hartley, and Tina Hartley. How do you plead?"

"Not guilty," Crawley said.

"Mr. Carrington," Panghorn turned to the plaintiff's table. "You may proceed."

"Thank you, your honor," Carrington stood up. "I call my first witness, Mr. Eddie Ballard."

Eddie approached the judge's table. His cane tapped along the floor. Frank directed him and held out a bible. He placed a hand on it.

"Mr. Ballard," Frank said. "Do you swear to tell the truth, the whole truth, and nothing but the truth?"

"I do," Eddie replied. Frank led him into the witness chair.

"Mr. Ballard," Carrington walked over to him. "Can you tell the jury what you heard at Littler's hardware?"

"I heard some men call for Mr. Littler," Eddie said. "They mentioned him by name, and talked about outstanding taxes, which I figured was some kind of protection money."

"Objection!" Mr. Gregory shouted. "Speculative."

"Objection sustained," The judge said.

"Was there an argument?" Carrington asked.

"Yes," Eddie said. "I heard a heated conversation about taxes. I heard Littler confront them. One was referred to as Crawley. Another man present was referred to as Fate. They argued, and then the shooting started. I heard Fate try to talk Mr. Littler into surrendering. He mentioned that his son Pete had been shot in the fight. Mal agreed. Then I heard another shot."

"Can you talk about the events that happened over the next couple of days?" Carrington asked.

"I heard a marshal was in town, and I came forward to give a statement," Eddie continued. "I was taken to the hotel by Deputy Whitmore, and we were attacked on the street. I got knocked over and heard shooting. Then that night I was woken up to the smell of smoke.

Mr. Whitmore said there was a fire and got me out. We moved to a hotel in Granite, but they stopped me from eating my supper after a dog apparently died from eating a scrap from the plate. Then some men started shooting downstairs as I was in my room.

Someone came in and I stayed put. I knew it wasn't Joe after I heard the deputy outside challenge them, only to be shot. I felt somebody grab me and pull a gun to my head. Joe came in and demanded he surrender and then shot him."

"Mr. Ballard, I understand you are blind and therefore could not recognize the defendant's face," Carrington said. "But would you be able to recognize the defendant's voice?"

"I would," Eddie nodded.

Carrington turned to Crawley. "Mr. Crawley, I'd like you to say something. Can you say 'Are you out there, Littler'?"

"Objection!" Mr. Gregory stood up. "Relevance."

"I wish to put a voice to words, your honor," Carrington said.

"Objection overruled," the judge said. "Proceed, Mr. Carrington."

"Mr. Crawley, if you please," The prosecutor stared at him.

"Fine," Crawley stood up and cleared his throat. "Are you out there, Littler?"

His voice echoed through the dining room. Joe noticed Eddie tense up as he heard it.

"Mr. Ballard," Carrington adjusted his bowtie. "Was that the voice you heard when the shooting took place?"

"Yes," Eddie replied. The spectators gasped.

"You may ask, Mr. Gregory," Carrington sat down.

***

Daisy Hartley took the oath and sat down in the witness chair.

"Mrs. Hartley," Carrington said, "Can you describe what took place at Littler's Hardware on the day of the incident?"

"My daughter and I were buying some supplies," Daisy said after taking a deep breath. "I was chatting with Mr. Littler, when Pete called him over to the window. Mr. Crawley was approaching the store with his foreman, introduced as Lafayette Bullock, and two other men."

"Did you believe there was going to be a confrontation?" Carrington asked.

"Objection!" Mr. Gregory shouted. "Leading!"

"Sustained," Panghorn said.

"Can you tell us what happened when Pete saw the men?" Carrington mopped his brow with a handkerchief.

"Yes," Daisy nodded. "Mr. Littler told us to stay inside. He gave Pete a shotgun and stepped outside. I peered out of the window. Mr. Bullock talked about taxes that Mr. Littler owed, and Mr. Littler accused Mr. Crawley of demanding protection money. They argued, and Crawley spoke of showing the townspeople that they couldn't take liberties."

"What happened next?" Carrington asked.

"I heard Mr. Littler shout 'Wait!', and then the shooting started," Daisy buried her face in her hands.

"Mrs. Hartley," Carrington rested a hand on her shoulder. "I know this is difficult, but I need you tell me what happened next."

"I hid against the floor with my daughter as the shooting started," Tears poured down her face. "When it stopped, I peered out again. There was a lot of smoke. I heard Mr. Bullock call out for Mr. Littler. I didn't see Pete, but I heard Mr. Littler. He set his guns on the ground and asked Mr. Littler to come out and meet with him."

"And did he?" Carrington asked.

"Yes," Daisy nodded. "Mr. Littler stepped out, and then I heard a shot. I saw Mr. Crawley walk into view, holding a smoking gun. As Mr. Littler fell to the ground, I saw Mr. Crawley walk over and shoot him in the head."

"You may ask, Mr. Gregory," Carrington sat down.

"Mrs. Hartley," Crawley's defense stood up. "You said that Mr. Littler gave his son a shotgun before heading outside to speak to Mr. Crawley."

"Yes," Daisy aimed a worried glance at Carrington.

"And you said you heard Mr. Littler shout 'Wait!' before the shooting started?"

"Yes."

"According to my client's deposition," Mr. Gregory produced a sheet of paper. "Mr. Littler was talking to his son, who had cocked the shotgun when the voices began to raise."

"I didn't hear a gun being cocked," Daisy stared him down.

"Did you see Mr. Littler's son from the window?" Gregory asked.

"No," Daisy said.

Joe watched as Mr. Gregory looked back at Mr. Crawley."

"Thank you, Mrs. Hartley," he said. "No further questions."

Daisy left the witness chair and returned to the plaintiff's table.

"Your honor," Carrington said, "As you can see, we can place Mr. Crawley at the scene of the murder. To demonstrate his motive, I would like to tie him to an incident of extortion. I call my next witness, Mr. Silas Coffey."

Silas heaved himself out of his chair. Amy helped him to the bench. After swearing the oath, he sat in the witness chair.

"Mr. Coffey," Carrington said, "could you state your occupation?"

"I own and operate a general store," Silas replied. "Not long after opening, Mr. Crawley came by and demanded a 'tax'. He said that all businesses were required to pay it. I refused, sensing it wasn't legitimate. Not long afterwards, I had regular incidents. Windows being broken. Drunk men harassing my daughter. They even tried to make me walk without my crutch."

"Did you have any association with Mr. Littler?" Carrington asked.

"Yes," Silas said. "We were friends."

"Did Mr. Littler talk about similar incidents?"

"Yes. He said he'd refused to pay the tax as well."

"Thank you, Mr. Coffey."

***

Joe's legs were stiff as the trial continued. More shopkeepers came forward and spoke out against Crawley. The judge turned to the assembled jury after they returned from their deliberations.

"Mr. Foreman," he asked. "Do you have a verdict?"

"Guilty on all charges, your honor," the juror replied, amid gasps from the spectators.

"Very well," Panghorn stared at Crawley. "Hudson Crawley, this court has found you guilty of extortion, the murder of Malcom and Pete Littler, and conspiracy to murder Eddie Ballard, Daisy Hartley, and Tina Hartley. You are hereby sentenced to be taken from this place and hanged by the neck until dead. May God have mercy on your soul. This sentence is to take place immediately."

He struck his gavel against the table. Excited murmurs arose amongst the spectators.

Lester and Frank led Crawley outside. Joe followed them as they put the condemned man on a horse and bound his hands behind his back. They mounted their own horses and led Crawley to the old tree Joe had seen when he had first arrived in Leadville. He noticed the undertaker and his carpenters walking alongside him. The undertaker carried a length of rope.

"You're the hangman too?" Joe raised an eyebrow. The undertaker nodded.

The undertaker walked over to the tree and fashioned a noose. He handed it to Frank, who placed the noose around Crawley's neck.

"Any last words?" the marshal asked.

"Don't think you and your bulldog have done your good deed for the day," Crawley said. "Without my oversight, this town will descend into chaos. You've put a lot of folks out of a job, and they're gonna want to get even."

Amy tightened her grip on Joe's hand as she listened to Crawley's words. He looked into her eyes, turning away from the hanging tree. As he embraced her, he heard Frank slap Crawley's horse. It whinnied and galloped away. The rope creaked as it went taut. The spectators gasped and then applauded.

"Come on," Joe said. "Let's get away from here. Watching a fellow swing ain't my kind of spectacle."

"Agreed," Amy said.

They weaved through the gathered crowd. Joe removed his hat and held it to his chest.

Epilogue

Joe sat on the porch outside Coffey's General Store, watching the sunset. Amy leaned on the rail next to him.

"How are you feeling?" Amy asked.

"Gonna be resting up for a week," Joe laid a hand on his bandaged torso. "But I should feel like my old self again after that."

"And not a moment too soon," Silas hobbled outside. "What did you think about Crawley's last words?"

"He's got a point," Joe said. "Even with him gone, this is a rough town. With that in mind, I reckon I ought to hang around."

"I think Amy would be happy about that," Silas winked. She fidgeted.

Joe looked at them both. "You know about us, don't you?"

"Mr. Whitmore," Silas patted him on the shoulder. "You're not the kind of suitor I would pick for my daughter. However, she's an adult and decides for herself. I'm happy for you both."

"Thanks," Joe hauled himself to his feet, wincing at the exertion. "That means a lot. I think I'm in debt to both of you for everything you've done."

"Don't mention it," Silas raised a hand. "It was the least we could do for you, stepping in when those thugs were causing trouble."

Frank approached the porch, carrying a bottle of whiskey.

"I thought I'd find you here," He uncorked the bottle and handed it to Joe. "I gotta head back to my office in Denver soon. Got a whole backlog of outlaws I gotta bring in. But I figured I owed you a drink for helping bring Crawley to justice."

"What's gonna happen to his little empire?" Joe took a swig from the bottle and handed it back to Frank.

"The Crawley Ranch and the Crawley Mining Company are now owned by the federal government," Frank took a swig and offered it to Silas and Amy, who declined. "Reckon they're gonna be up for auction soon. Might even be a land grant in it for anybody who wants to try working the land."

"I don't have the money for that," Joe chuckled. "Besides, I ain't a miner."

"You'll make a good lawman," Frank grinned.

"I doubt that," Joe replied. "Speaking of which."

He removed the deputy marshal's badge from his lapel and offered it to Frank.

"You're turning in your badge?" Frank raised an eyebrow.

"I figured you'd want it back," Joe said. "My work here's done. I'm looking at new lines of work. Preferably something that doesn't involve pointing guns at folk. Badge or no badge."

"Well, if you ain't a miner or a ranch hand, what do you have in mind?" Frank asked.

Joe exchanged a smile with Silas and Amy. Frank aimed glances between them.

"Well, I'm real happy for you," Frank shook Joe's hand. "You'll make a crackerjack store clerk. And if you ever change your mind, come and find me in Denver."

"Thanks for the offer," Joe said, "but I kinda like it here."

"The sheriff ain't walking yet either," Frank replied. "He could use a deputy if you want something local. You'll even get a cut of the county taxes. Then maybe you can spend some of that money on a stake in a mines or ranch."

"I'll think about it," Joe said. "So long, Frank. Maybe you'll visit this town again sometime."

"Maybe I will," Frank smiled. "Good luck out there, Joe. Ma'am."

He tipped his hat to Amy and walked back towards the saloon.

Joe watched his friend leave.

"Penny for your thoughts?" Amy said.

"Just thinking about the future," Joe put his arm around her. "Do you think I should be the deputy sheriff?"

"You're good with a gun and you have a reputation," Amy replied. "Folks might be more willing to back down when faced by the man who stared down Fate."

"Guess that's a reputation I gotta be able to uphold," Joe massaged his forehead. "But I'll deal with that when it happens. And it will happen. That's something you gotta be aware of."

"I ain't afraid of that," Amy said. "We knew the risks when we moved here. And I feel a lot safer with you around."

"To be honest, this town needs some decent law and order," Silas said. "I've seen plenty of folks going through what you went through, Joe. Once you've killed, you feel you gotta be a soldier for the rest of your days. Having a badge could be the way to do it. If you can bring folks in without killing them, that's the real challenge."

Joe paused. He turned to Amy. "What do you think, darling?"

"I'd love to see you working as a clerk," she replied. "We could use the help and it might keep you out of trouble. And I'd miss you if you went back to Denver with Marshal Buchanan. But Daddy's right. This town is a rough place and needs some decent law. You gotta do what you gotta do. And whichever path you take, I'll support you."

Joe nodded and gave her a warm smile.

The sound of gunshots echoed down the street, followed by a scream.

"That sounds like it came from the mining camp!" Silas peered over the railing.

The two shopkeepers turned towards Joe, both giving him an expectant stare. He looked back at them, and then towards the mining camp.

"I gotta do what I gotta do." He tightened his gun belt and walked towards the camp.

The End

Thanks for taking the time to read this story. A positive review on Amazon would be appreciated.